"Melissa's been accepted to Smith College, Will,"
explained to Will. "Her *'dream school.'*"

Will felt a strange thud inside his chest. Melissa
was going to Smith? When did that happen? And
when had she been planning to tell him all this? Not
that it mattered now. But still. If this had been in the
works all along, did it mean she'd never planned on
being with him after graduation?

For years they had talked about going off to the
same college. They'd planned to stay in dorms the
first couple of years and then maybe rent a place together—if they could get her parents to agree to it.

Get over it, he told himself. *Obviously Liss is moving on. Why can't you?*

Suddenly Will remembered something—the letter from NYU. He *was* moving on. All the way to the
Big Apple, in fact. He smiled. Then he sat forward
and cleared his throat. "Hey, guys. Speaking of college, I've got some news."

"What?" Josh asked. The others grew silent and
stared at him expectantly.

Will took a deep breath and said, "I got accepted
to New York University."

If Melissa thought she could just run off to an
East Coast school and totally blow off everything,
fine. She wasn't the only one.

Don't miss any of the books in SWEET VALLEY HIGH
SENIOR YEAR, an exciting series from Bantam Books!

Visit the Official Sweet Valley Web Site on the Internet at:

www.sweetvalley.com

Francine Pascal's SVH senioryear

It Takes Two

CREATED BY
FRANCINE PASCAL

BANTAM BOOKS
NEW YORK · TORONTO · LONDON · SYDNEY · AUCKLAND

RL: 6, AGES 012 AND UP

IT TAKES TWO
A Bantam Book / July 2002

Sweet Valley High® is a registered trademark of Francine Pascal.
Conceived by Francine Pascal.
Cover photography by Michael Segal.

Produced by 17th Street Productions,
an Alloy, Inc. company.
151 West 26th Street
New York, NY 10011.

ISBN: 0-553-49392-2

Visit us on the Web! www.randomhouse.com/teens

Published simultaneously in the United States and Canada

Bantam Books is an imprint of Random House Children's Books, a
division of Random House, Inc. BANTAM BOOKS and the rooster
colophon are registered trademarks of Random House, Inc. Bantam Books,
1540 Broadway, New York, New York 10036.

PRINTED IN THE UNITED STATES OF AMERICA

OPM   0 9 8 7 6 5 4 3 2 1

To Matthew Markowitz

Will Simmons

Whipped. Wuss.

I'm tired of being called stuff like that. Okay, let me be honest . . . I'm tired of _being_ a whipped wuss. Melissa thinks she can completely mess with my life, then snap her fingers and I'll crawl right back to her. And why wouldn't she think that? I always have in the past.

But not this time. This time she's gone too far.

Jessica Wakefield

Ditz. Space cadet. Total flake.

Why do people always see me as a dumb blonde? Even my brother nicknamed me "Airhead." You know what — I think it's all Elizabeth's fault. Just because she was born an ultraresponsible, control-freaky list maker, I look like a slacker in comparison.

Well, lately Liz has been the ditz, too caught up in Jeff to think about much else. So maybe now people will finally see that I do have a brain.

melissa Fox

Conniving witch?
Sure, that's probably now
some people see me. But I
prefer a different term: survivor.

CHAPTER 1
Berkeley's Poster Boy

Melissa somehow managed to get from her car to her front door, even though she could barely feel her feet moving. Her heart was pounding like crazy, but it still didn't seem to be getting any blood to the rest of her body.

She opened the door and stepped into the foyer. Catching her reflection in the mirror above the wooden console, she turned to face herself and the events of the past fifteen minutes.

Okay. So they caught me. She had worked up such a brilliant plan to get back at Will for fooling around behind her back, and the whole thing had just blown up in her face. Why hadn't she seen that ambush coming?

Stupid football loyalty. She'd totally overlooked that minor detail. For some reason, when guys bashed their heads together on a sports field, they bonded for life. That must have been it. Aaron definitely wanted her, but obviously not enough to cross Will. So he set her up to get busted.

1

"Fine," she said, scowling at her reflection. So what if her plan didn't work out? She wasn't going to let Will make her feel bad. He'd brought this whole thing on himself by messing around with Erika Brooks. Besides, she had loyal friends too. Well, maybe not Cherie, now that she'd witnessed that little moment with Aaron, the love of Cherie's five minutes, but the other girls would do anything she asked. And as soon as she told them her side of the story, they'd totally back her up. Then she could figure out a new way to get revenge, and this time she wouldn't miss a single detail.

Right now Will thought he had the upper hand, but he was wrong. He was the guilty one—not her. The whole point of messing around with Aaron was to make him understand how it felt to see her with someone else. She wanted him to drown in the same frantic, helpless anger she'd been dealing with. That awful image of him locking lips with Erika was still burned in her mind.

But no, she wouldn't think about that right now. In fact, she didn't want to think about anything upsetting. The longer she could put off her emotions, the more in control she would be. It was time to focus on something else.

Like frozen yogurt. Raspberry-almond swirl.

That was definitely what she needed. Leaving her

car keys on the hall table, Melissa rounded the corner and headed into the kitchen. As she slipped off her backpack and hung it from one of the tall wooden chairs, she noticed a bulging manila envelope on the breakfast table. It was addressed to her, from Smith College in Massachusetts. She picked it up and tore it open. A letter on thick, crisp stationery slipped out into her grasp.

Dear Ms. Fox,

We are pleased to inform you that you have been selected for enrollment at our college beginning this fall. Your application showed you to be a hardworking, dedicated, well-rounded individual who we feel will be an asset to our student community. Thank you for choosing Smith College. We look forward to seeing you this September.

Huh. Melissa squinted, staring at the words for a second. Then she shoved the letter back into the envelope and tossed it aside before strolling over to the freezer.

She knew she should be more excited that a major East Coast school wanted her, but for some reason, it didn't feel like a big deal. She and Will had definitely decided to go to a California school, and she'd only applied to Smith as a backup, just to see if she could get in. Kind of the same way Aaron was just supposed to be an ego boost—a cute guy she could use to get back at Will, but nothing serious.

Melissa cringed. At least Smith had accepted her, though. They didn't go calling up UCLA to tell them they weren't her only choice.

Evan Plummer stood in the middle of his kitchen, rummaging through the mail.

Bill, catalog, another bill, ad for a big HDTV sale, coupon booklet . . . man, how many trees died every day to create this junk? At the bottom of the pile was a brown-paper envelope, addressed to him. The return address bore the University of California at Berkeley logo.

Evan's heart accelerated. It was here. *Finally.*

He fumbled with the envelope, trying to get it open. His fingers were shaking, but eventually he managed to tear off an end. Taking a deep breath, Evan yanked out the contents and quickly scanned the beginning of the letter.

Dear Mr. Plummer:
    Thank you for applying to our institution. We are sorry to inform you that enrollment for our fall semester is at full capacity and

4

*your name has been added to our waiting list.
Should an opening arise, you will be contacted
as soon as possible.*

The words began to blur as Evan felt a full-body shiver. Then he quickly clenched his fists, crumpling the paper. *This can't be happening,* he thought, shaking his head. He'd been planning to go to Berkeley since he was ten years old! It was the only place he wanted to go. What was he supposed to do now?

As if on autopilot, Evan's arm reached for the phone on the wall. In a daze he punched Jade's number.

"Hello?"

Evan leaned against the wall and shut his eyes. "Jade?" For some reason his mouth was incredibly dry.

"Evan? Is that you? What's wrong?"

For a split second he didn't want to answer. It was bad enough just *knowing.* Saying it aloud would make it worse—more real.

But he had to tell sometime. Besides, he really wanted Jade's help. Taking a deep breath, Evan pushed the words out. "Berkeley turned me down."

"What?" She sounded even worse than he did. "Are you sure?"

"I got the letter today," he said. "The whole we're-sorry-to-inform-you part was pretty clear."

Jade sighed loudly. "I just don't get it. Why wouldn't

they want you? You're perfect for that school."

"Yeah, well, that's what I thought," Evan replied, trying not to sound bitter and failing badly. He turned and rested his forehead against the wall. The buzzing fluorescent lights of the kitchen seemed unusually harsh. He had a strange urge to morph into a giant sea turtle and disappear into the darkness and quiet of a snug shell.

Sea turtles. One of his recent projects had been to try to raise awareness about the endangered status of the creatures. In fact, he was hoping to spend more time at Berkeley studying the situation and trying to preserve their habitat. Now he wouldn't be able to help them. Not there.

Was this how it was going to be from now on? Every single thought leading him in a circle?

"So they just said no, like that?" Jade asked. "Nothing else?"

Evan paused, glancing over at the crumpled letter. "Well, you know, they said I'm on the waiting list. But that means nothing."

"The *waiting* list? Evan, that's not the same thing as being rejected," Jade argued. "It means you might still get in. You know what? I bet what they didn't say is that you're at *the top* of the waiting list. I mean, you're like a poster boy for their college. They've *got to* let you in."

As Jade rambled on, Evan stared at the opposite wall. It was nice of Jade to try and make him feel better, but talking about the situation meant he had to think about it. And all he wanted to do was shut down his brain and pretend it didn't happen.

A loud clicking noise suddenly interrupted Jade's ranting.

"Uh . . . Jade? Is that your other line?" Evan mumbled, glad to focus on something else.

"Yeah. I'll ignore it."

"No. Go ahead. It's okay."

As she switched lines, Evan slid down onto the floor. He felt completely drained, like he couldn't imagine ever having any energy again.

"Evan?" Jade's voice came back on the phone.

"Yeah?"

"That was Tia. She and Andy are heading to House of Java, and they want us to meet them."

Evan rubbed his right temple with his free hand. "I don't know," he said.

"Hey, I know you're not feeling great," she began, "but you know, moping around your house is only going to drive you crazy. Maybe we should go out and *do* something."

Evan exhaled slowly, his hand moving down to rub the back of his neck. He really, really didn't want to be social right now. But Jade was right. If he stayed at home and kept obsessing about all this, he'd probably lose his grip.

"Fine," he said. "But promise me something, okay? Don't tell them about Berkeley turning me down. I just don't want anyone else to know yet."

"I know. I promise," Jade replied. "I'll call them back and tell them we're on our way. In the meantime *try not to think about Berkeley!*"

"Yeah, right," Evan muttered after he'd hung up the phone.

Why couldn't she have asked him to do something easier? Like, "Try not to breathe anymore"?

Will Simmons sped his Chevy Blazer up the driveway, jerked it into park, and turned off the engine. He tried to throw open the door and shut it with a therapeutic slam, but it got stuck and he had to throw his weight against it to push it open.

He glared at the door, then slammed it as hard as he could, but it wasn't nearly as satisfying as he'd hoped.

He hated that car.

Banging open the side door, he marched into the house and headed straight for the kitchen. What he needed was some peace and quiet and a glass of cold soda. Scanning the contents of the refrigerator, he suddenly remembered that he'd had the last can of soda yesterday. All that was in there now was juice.

"Great," he grumbled as he shut the fridge. He hated juice.

Will hated everything right now. His car, the contents of the fridge, and—most of all—a certain lying, cheating, evil ex-girlfriend whose name he was never going to think about again.

"Where's Melissa?"

Will spun around and frowned at his mother. "Mom! Do you have to sneak up on me like that?"

She laughed. "Oh, I'm sorry," she said, tucking the front of her blond bob behind her ears. "So where is she?"

"Who cares?" Will snapped. "Do you think I'm supposed to do everything with her? Can't I come home and grab a snack without checking in with her first?"

Mrs. Simmons raised her eyebrows. "Excuse me," she said. "I only asked because you usually bring her home with you after practice."

Will winced. He'd been ready to blow ever since he'd suffered the humiliation of witnessing his so-called girlfriend come on to one of his friends that afternoon. His mom had just been in the wrong place at the wrong time.

"Well, I can see you're in a bad mood, so I won't bother you anymore," his mother said. She paused, and her eyes took on a strange, knowing gleam. "I just came in to tell you that you got some *mail* today.

It's on the counter over there next to the grocery bag." She watched him another second longer, still smiling, then left the room. What was with her? Since when did his mom let him snap at her without getting upset?

Curious, Will walked over to see what mail she was talking about. It was a large white envelope, addressed to him. He glanced at the return address, and then he realized why his mom had been acting so weird. The package was from New York University.

He'd almost forgotten he'd even applied there. It had only been a couple of months ago, but somehow it felt like longer. Almost as if it had been someone else. Will snatched up the packet and ripped it open, pulling out the cover letter. He skimmed over the words.

. . . thank you for applying to . . . happy to inform . . . chosen for admission beginning this fall semester . . .

"Yes!" Will exclaimed, raising a fist in the air. He could feel all his tension morph into enthusiasm.

This was perfect. Ever since he got into sports journalism, he'd been into the idea of going to NYU, a school with a great writing program that also happened to be in a city with some of the best teams in every major sport. But somehow Melissa had talked him out of seriously considering NYU, making him believe California was where they belonged. He'd still applied, just as a backup. Good thing too. Now he had an escape route—something to focus on other than the mess and melodrama he was in at the moment. Forget Melissa and their too long, too insane past. Now there was nothing to prevent him from filling out the acceptance form that very moment and mailing it back to them.

Will snatched a pen out of the nearby junk drawer and plopped down at the kitchen table. He sat for a moment, pondering the crisp, clean white form, with all its neat blank lines. It was like staring at a map—his path away from Melissa. All he had to do was fill it out and send it. Then he'd be free. But for some reason, he just couldn't bring himself to write anything.

"It's this stupid pen," he said, squinting at the fuzzy tip of his black ballpoint. He reached over and grabbed another pen from the drawer, one with a cleaner point. But as he hunched back over the paper, he still couldn't make a single mark. The more he looked at the document, the more ominous it seemed. *Name!* it screamed in big black letters. *Social Security Number!* Will rested his forehead against his fingertips and was surprised to find that he was sweating.

"Forget it!" he cried, throwing the pen down.

Maybe it was just too soon. His brain must still be reeling from the whole Melissa saga. If he gave himself a day to recover, he'd be able to do it, no problem. After all, this was extremely important. He needed to be able to concentrate and do a good job.

"Tomorrow," he said, refolding the letter.

Will shoved the paper back into the envelope. Yeah, today was just too soon. He'd be more prepared to deal with it tomorrow. Or maybe the next day. Definitely sometime this week . . .

"*You're* getting an espresso?" Andy exclaimed as Evan reached across House of Java's front counter to hand Jessica a five-dollar bill. "But I thought you only imbibed the unfiltered juice of the roots of organic, native-growing plants!"

Evan rolled his eyes. "Hey, I drink coffee," he said. "But only if the beans are picked by unionized farmworkers who are paid regulated wages and get health benefits."

"They have that kind of coffee here?" Tia asked.

"We do now," Jessica remarked as she handed Evan his change. "Evan kept pushing the point on our poor manager. So now Ally keeps a couple of bags of union-grown beans under the counter for when he comes in. Of course it means I have to grind them and refill the machine with his stuff, so it takes a while."

"So it's not really an espresso, is it? It's more of a 'wait-in-line-o,'" Andy quipped. "Hey, I like that. I should write it down for my next routine. You got a pen, Tia?"

As Tia and Andy muttered together, Jade reached

12

over and squeezed Evan's hand. He looked at her and forced a grin. He knew she was checking up on him, making sure he was okay, and he wanted her to think he was fine.

"Okay, here you go," Jessica announced, pushing a tray toward them. "One mocha latte, two cappuccinos, and one cup of guilt-free coffee." She grinned at Evan as they each grabbed their drinks.

"So since when are you keeping notes for routines, Andy?" Jade asked as they walked to the back of the café and sat down at a small table.

"Since today," Andy replied with a proud smile. "I got tired of thinking up all this great stuff and then forgetting it, so I've started this writing-down system. Look." He reached into his jacket pocket and pulled out what looked like a wad of trash. "This napkin is stuff I jotted down at lunch. This was during homeroom. And all these notes are from government class. I hate government class."

"Let me see." Tia reached over, smoothed out one of the papers, and read, "'Because they have two noses.' That sounds funny," she said, grinning at Andy. "What's it about?"

Andy peered over her shoulder at the paper. "Oh . . . um . . . I forget."

"What about this one?" Jade reached for another scrap. "'The hamburgers are toasted!'"

13

Andy's frown deepened. "Hmmm. Yeah, I forget that one too." He rummaged through the pile of papers. "Great. I can't remember any of these. I guess I should write down more than just the punch lines, huh?"

Tia rolled her eyes at Jade, and the two of them burst out laughing. Evan smiled and sat back in his chair, taking a sip of his politically correct coffee. For the first time since he read the Berkeley letter, the shock was starting to wear off—just a little.

"Oh, man. This is hopeless," Andy whined, staring down at the row of scraps in front of him. "I guess it's a good thing I'm not planning on going straight to college, huh? Although I hear the comedy-club circuit has killer midterms."

"Can we please stay away from the *c* word?" Tia said, giving a little shudder.

Jade shot Evan a quick glance. "Yeah, can we?" she chimed in.

Andy frowned at Tia. "I don't get why you'd want to—shouldn't you be all jumping up and down about those acceptance letters you got?"

Tia bit her lip. "Of course I'm glad I'm getting into good schools, but it just means that I finally have to actually choose which one to accept. I mean, even if I defer for a year to do some volunteer work somewhere, I still have to make the decision about where I'll be going the next year—and I have to make it,

14

like, so soon." She looked over at Evan and Jade. "Isn't it freaking you guys out too? I just can't believe we're already here. This year has gone so fast."

Jade shifted uncomfortably. "Um, Tia? I thought we didn't want to talk about college stuff."

"Right. I'm sorry." Tia laughed awkwardly and shook her head. "It's just that my parents were already on my back after seeing my acceptance letters from Cal Tech and Pepperdine. And now today I got this acceptance letter from Berkeley—"

"What?" Evan sat up straight, his heart suddenly racing. "You got a letter from where?"

"From Berkeley," Tia repeated, barely glancing at him. "Anyway, it's great and all, but it just makes the decision harder because they're all good schools and I don't know which one is right for me."

Evan felt something building in his chest, pushing up until it nearly blocked his airway. Anger. Pure anger. "What do you mean 'you don't know'?" he snapped.

Tia raised her eyebrows. "I mean: *I . . . don't . . . know.*"

"But . . ." He clenched his fists so hard, he could almost feel his finger joints fusing. Was this for real? His friend had been handed the opportunity he would have given anything for, and she wasn't even sure if she *wanted* it?

"Um . . . so what do you guys think about Mrs.

Loomis's new dye job?" Jade asked a little too loudly. "Doesn't she look like a psychotic Elmo or something?"

"Wait a minute. Wait a minute." Evan leaned across the table toward Tia, completely ignoring Jade. "Berkeley is, like, one of *the* best schools in the country. How could you not want to go there?"

Tia sighed. "Of course I want to go there. Just like I want to go to all the schools I've heard back from! How do I choose?" She narrowed her eyes at him. "Why is this such a big deal to you anyway?"

Evan flinched, then slumped back in his seat as the anger was replaced by the deflation he'd been feeling ever since he saw his rejection letter. "Look, I'm sorry," he said. "It's just that . . . Berkeley was my first choice. My *only* choice. And I just got a letter today saying they've turned me down. I'm on the waiting list, but that's not so promising."

"Oh." Tia's brown eyes filled with pity. "I'm really sorry, Evan."

"It's okay. It's not your fault or anything," he mumbled, wishing he'd never said anything. Now everyone was staring at him like he was a big loser. Which, actually, wasn't so far from the truth.

melissa Fox

6:37 P.M.

Hey, Gina, since when do you
not answer your cell? It's melissa.
Give me a call. I've got to tell you
about something. It's important.

7:55 P.M.

amy, it's melissa. Do you know
where Gina is? Give me a call
when you guys get back from the
mall or whatever. It's serious.

9:43 P.M.

Lila. Hey, it's melissa. are
you with Gina or amy? Call me,
okay? It's crucial we talk
immediately. Oh, and if cherie
calls, just ignore her.

CHAPTER 2
The Only Responsible Wakefield Child

Evan sat on the floor across the hall from Mr. Nelson's office, waiting. And waiting. He crossed his legs Indian style and pressed his fingers to his temples. *Open!* he commanded mentally as he stared at the door. *Open now!* To his surprise, the door flew open. Jane Templeton, a senior from his homeroom class, started heading out.

"Thanks so much, Mr. Nelson!" she said over her shoulder. "I've dreamed of going to UCLA my whole life! I can't believe it's really going to happen!"

A burst of anger jetted up inside Evan. As Jane stepped into the hallway, he briefly considered sticking out his leg and tripping her.

Man. What's wrong with me? he wondered. *I'm so against violence, yet lately all I want to do is punch people in the nose.*

Mr. Nelson stepped into the doorway. "I'm happy to help, Jane," he said, shaking her hand. "You've worked very hard, and you deserve your success."

18

As Jane twirled around and practically skipped down the hall, Mr. Nelson turned toward Evan.

"Mr. Plummer?" he said, his bushy eyebrows lifting into two distinct semicircles. "What brings you by?"

Evan stood and glanced around him. "I, uh, need to talk to you," he mumbled.

"Come on in." Mr. Nelson pushed the door open wider and gestured into his office. Evan shoved his hands in his pockets and followed the guidance counselor inside.

Mr. Nelson walked around his desk and settled into his squeaky executive-style chair, and Evan plopped into the chair in front of the desk. Funny how he'd never really noticed the office decor until now. Hanging everywhere were university posters, mainly of California schools. Each one depicted a politically correct racial mix of students hanging out at some campus locale, holding open textbooks and smiling broadly. As Evan studied the walls, his gaze wandered onto one full-color print and stopped. *The University of California at Berkeley,* it read in giant red type. There were no perfectly posed undergraduates. No false smiles or textbook props. Just a shot of the Campanile, mocking him.

Evan felt another surge of anger.

"So what can I do for you?" Mr. Nelson asked, leaning back in his chair.

"I . . . um . . . I heard from Berkeley yesterday,"

Evan began, absently tugging on the frayed knees of his jeans. "They turned me down."

Mr. Nelson sat forward and leaned across his desk, a sympathetic-counselor's gaze taking over his features. "I'm sorry to hear that, Evan."

"They said I was put on the waiting list, but . . ." Evan paused and swallowed back a lump in his throat. "I was, you know, hoping for more."

"Have you heard from any other colleges?" Mr. Nelson asked, clasping his hands in front of him.

"No, actually. I'd kind of been banking on Berkeley coming through."

"I see." Mr. Nelson exhaled sharply. "Well, it's not too late to find another institution where you could receive a fine education." He reached down and pulled open a drawer.

"Wait," Evan blurted. "The reason I came here wasn't to find another college. I was wondering—is there anything I can do to still get into Berkeley?"

Mr. Nelson slowly shut the drawer and resumed his hands-clasped, I'm-so-understanding pose across the desk.

"It's just that I don't understand why they rejected me," Evan continued, running a hand through his dark hair. "I made it clear through my essay that I've worked hard for social change and was active in lots of service organizations."

"Well, it is true that you've devoted a lot of time toward good causes," Mr. Nelson said, nodding. "However, you have to remember that Berkeley, even though it might be known as a hotbed of liberal thinking, is still an institution of higher learning. Just like other colleges, it looks for applicants who are well-rounded as well as committed. You never worked as hard at making good grades as you did toward social change. And other than the environmental group and swimming, you were not very active in extracurricular *school* activities."

"Does Berkeley really care about stuff like that?" Evan asked.

"I'm afraid they do," Mr. Nelson replied.

"But that's . . . I mean, it's not like . . ." Evan shook his head. "It's just not fair," he finally mumbled. It was all he could say. It was the same phrase that had been echoing in his head since yesterday. His new mantra.

Mr. Nelson's chair groaned loudly as he leaned back. "You should be glad you got on the waiting list and didn't get a flat-out rejection," he said with a small smile. "There's still hope."

"Yeah, right," Evan muttered.

"People get moved up from waiting lists all the time. It depends mainly on how many of the students accepted end up not going for one reason or another." He swiveled his chair to the side and fiddled with a stack of papers on his desk. "For example, Berkeley typically won't admit more than three students from Sweet Valley High, and those spots are already taken. But if any of those students decides not to go to Berkeley, your chances of getting in improve a great deal. And the sooner they inform the college of their decision not to attend, the better for you."

Evan straightened. "Do you know if any of them aren't going?"

Mr. Nelson shrugged. "I really can't say. Berkeley is an excellent school, so it's not impossible that all three will accept."

"Okay. Well, thanks anyway," Evan mumbled as he got to his feet.

"Don't let this get you down, Evan. Like I said, there's still a chance. In the meantime it's a good idea for you to communicate with some other local schools while you wait to hear."

"Yeah, okay. I'll let you know." Evan turned and headed out of the office before Mr. Nelson could try any more counselor psychobabble on him. He really didn't want to think about any other schools—at least not yet. Berkeley had been all that mattered to him for so long.

So now his only hope was for one of three brainy students—including his own friend Tia—to turn Berkeley down, as soon as possible.

*   *   *

"Take it to the limit! Take it to the top! We're the Gladiators . . ."

"That's your cue, Fox. Run!" Coach Laufeld ordered.

Melissa took a running start, did a quick round off followed by a front flip, and finished off in splits formation directly in front of the other cheerleaders.

". . . and we can't be stopped!" she shouted, finishing the cheer. Unfortunately, her timing was slightly off and she ended up yelling "stopped" alone.

A chorus of snickering welled up behind her. Melissa didn't have to look to know who it was.

"Gotta hit those marks, Fox." Coach Laufeld shook her head. "And you're crowding the squad at the end. Give the girls more space when you tumble."

"Yes, *please*," came Cherie's loud whisper. Amy, Lila, and Gina giggled.

Melissa ignored the jittery feeling inside her and pretended to stretch out her leg muscles. She couldn't believe those witches were siding with Cherie. She'd fully expected Cherie to be in a snit over what happened with Aaron, but amazingly the girl managed to turn the rest of their friends against her too.

She'd been a little worried when no one returned her calls last night. Then she arrived at school that morning and found herself facing the silent treatment from every one of those cowards. She figured it would blow over after a while, but here it was the end of the day and things had only gotten worse. Now instead of just ignoring her, they were slamming her every chance they got.

"Is it just me, or is Melissa's skirt about three inches shorter than ours?" Cherie asked in a high-pitched, innocent-sounding voice.

"Of course!" Gina answered. "She's just advertising."

Melissa plastered a bored-looking expression on her face and acted like she couldn't hear them. She knew from experience that if they sensed any fear or humiliation from her, they'd only step it up a notch. Besides, it was surprisingly easy to blow them off. Their catty remarks weren't even all that original. Most of them she'd coined herself during the anti-Jessica campaign they'd launched earlier in the year, so they didn't even make a dent.

Still, she couldn't help feeling like a total loser not having anyone to talk to. Things were going to get really stressful if she didn't figure her way out of this.

Coach Laufeld blew her whistle and raised her hand in the air. "All right, girls. That's enough for today."

The squad immediately broke into small clusters and headed for the locker room. Melissa did a few more leg stretches before following them inside. But as soon as she came through the door, Cherie's red head snapped up and a new series of whispers began, followed by more rounds of laughter.

Melissa sauntered past them, her head held high, and sat down on a bench to unlace her sneakers. What did those airhead idiots know? They were going to end up as housewives or working at makeup counters in the mall. In the meantime *she'd* gotten an acceptance letter from Smith—if only she could wave it in their faces.

She froze in place, clutching her left sneaker. How had she missed it—she had exactly what it took to put them all in their place. She was going to go to Smith! She'd never seriously considered it before, but now it all made sense. There was nothing for her here anymore. Besides, Smith was a fantastic school, and they definitely wanted her. What did they call her? Hardworking? Dedicated? She'd be crazy to turn them down.

Melissa stood up straight and undid her ponytail, grinning as she fluffed out her hair. Funny how the answer had been so obvious all along. Forget high school and all this petty dramatic stuff. She was going to Smith College.

"Thinks she's so hot," someone hissed in her direction, probably Lila.

"I know. Will must be *so* glad to be rid of her," Cherie added loudly. "He's *so* much better off now."

Melissa felt a sharp pain in her chest. She paused while buttoning up her shirt, took a breath, and started again. Hopefully they didn't notice.

It doesn't matter, she told herself. *I'm beyond all this. A few more months and I won't even remember Will's name.* As she pulled on her suede skirt, she visualized the thick, glossy Smith catalog she had sitting on her desk at home. Hundreds of courses were listed inside—hundreds of ways to forget Will Simmons and these jerks she used to call her friends.

"It's just so hard! I'm starting to go into major freak-out mode."

Melissa glanced to her left and saw Tia pacing in front of a nearby bench. Jessica sat on one end, shaking her head sympathetically.

"I mean, one minute I'm thinking Berkeley would be the perfect place for me, and the next minute I can't even imagine myself there," Tia went on. "And I don't know how to make up my mind!"

"But you still have time, right?" Jessica asked. "You don't have to decide now, do you?"

"No," Tia replied, sitting next to Jessica. "I just hope I have more of a clue by the time the deadline comes."

Melissa smiled. Here was her chance.

"Hey, Tia," she said, turning to her left. "Did you say you got accepted to Berkeley?"

Tia and Jessica blinked back at her, obviously thrown by her sudden interest in them. Even Cherie and the gang grew silent.

"Yeah," Tia replied.

"Congratulations," Melissa said in her sincerest-sounding voice. "I hear it's a great school."

"Uh . . . thanks," Tia said, exchanging a quick glance with Jessica.

"I'm going to Smith College in Massachusetts," Melissa went on, propping her right foot on the bench to buckle her boot. "It's my dream school. I can't wait to get started there."

Out of the corner of her eye she could see Cherie, Gina, Lila, and Amy all look at one another in surprise. *Score.* Now they'd know they couldn't hurt her. They'd know she was moving on to bigger, better things.

"That's, um . . ." Tia shrugged slightly. "That's great, Melissa. Congrats."

Melissa grinned broadly. "Thanks," she said.

"So, who wants to go out to First and Ten?" Cherie asked loudly, standing and facing Gina, Lila, and Amy. Before they could reply, she cocked her head and added, "Oh, come on. All the guys are going. Aaron, Matt, Josh—*and Will.*"

"Will is going? Count me in," Lila said, standing.

Gina jumped to her feet. "Me too."

"I'm there," Amy added.

Melissa's stomach clenched. Still, why should she care what any of her friends did or even if it involved her ex-boyfriend?

Forget them, she told herself. *I'm above all this now.* Then she shut her eyes and imagined herself strolling through Smith College's lush green campus.

"Hello?" Jade's singsongy voice filled Evan's ear as he flopped down on his bed, holding on to the phone.

"Hey," he muttered.

"Hey, Evan," she said, her voice instantly morphing into a sympathetic tone. "I missed you at lunch."

"Yeah. Sorry. I skipped it so I could track down Nelson and get the scoop on why Berkeley shot me down."

"Really? What'd he say?"

Evan rolled onto his back. "He wasn't much help."

"I'm sorry," Jade said softly. "Have you told your parents yet?"

"No," Evan grunted.

"Um . . . not to be bossy or anything, but shouldn't you tell them pretty soon?"

"Yeah, yeah," Evan mumbled, rubbing his eyes with his free hand. "I will. But first I want to figure out what I'm going to do about it. They'll probably want to know that."

"Right," Jade said. "So what about Nelson? Didn't he have any kind of advice?"

"He said I should be glad I got on the waiting list. And he said if any of the three Sweet Valley students who got accepted ends up turning Berkeley down, my chances of getting in should go up."

Jade gave a slight gasp. "Well, that's it, then! This is perfect!"

"What?" Evan sat up. "What's perfect?"

"Look. We know that Tia is one of those three people, right?"

"Right." He knew where she was going—he'd already gone there. But how could he try and tell one of his best friends to give up Berkeley for him?

"And we know that she's not sure if she even wants to go, right?"

"Right," he said again. That was true—she wasn't nearly as hooked on going there was he was. So maybe . . .

"So, since Berkeley was your only choice and Tia obviously has plenty of options, she should hand her spot over to you. It's that simple."

Evan stood and paced around his bedroom. "Well, actually it's not *that* simple. I wouldn't automatically get her spot just because she opted out."

"But Mr. Nelson said it would really improve your odds, right?"

"Yeah."

"Well, then? Why not do everything you can to up your chances?"

Evan could feel his spirits starting to lift, but he forced them back down. He didn't want to get his hopes up—not yet.

"I don't know, Jade," he said. "Are you sure I wouldn't be a supreme jerk to ask Tia to do that for me?"

"Are you kidding? Of course not. She'd be the jerk if she actually said no, which there's no way she would do. Oh, wait—hold on a second." Evan could make out the sound of a muffled conversation in the background. "I've got to go," she said when she came back on the phone. "Mom's finally come out of her bedroom and wants us to go out to dinner. Lately she's been spending way too much time in there working on something. It's been nothing but fast food around this place for a whole week. But don't worry. I'm just saying no to any beef raised on clear-cut rain-forest land."

"Good girl."

"Bye, Evan. Promise me you'll think about asking Tia."

"I will," he said softly. "Bye."

Evan hung up the phone and plopped back down on his bed. He'd be thinking about it, all right. In fact, he probably wouldn't think of anything else.

* * *

Next Thursday . . . Next Thursday . . .

Jessica shut her leather-bound organizer and stared up at the ceiling. Why would next Thursday be important?

So much for staying on top of things. She had bought the beautiful black-leather organizer at the start of the semester, hoping to use it faithfully. After all, it was the end of her senior year in high school—she was almost a full-fledged adult—and she wanted to keep better track of all the important details in her life. Unfortunately, after making a few notes on the calendar and master to-do list, she'd promptly lost the organizer. She'd found it this afternoon in an empty shoe box while searching for her black-suede stilettos. Flipping through the pages, she discovered she had circled next Thursday's date for some reason. It rang familiar to her, but she wasn't sure why.

She reopened the organizer, hoping to find more clues. Let's see . . . there was a reminder to buy more Sedona Wild Plum lipstick (duh—like she'd forget that). She'd also marked the date when a really cool DVD hit the stores (bought it, watched it, already lost it). And . . . shoot—she'd missed the weekend Kismet Clothing Boutique had their annual anniversary sale!

Wait a second . . . Something stirred inside Jessica's memory. Anniversary? That was it!

"Oh, no!" she blurted. The organizer fell from

her lap onto a pile of clothes. "Next Thursday is Mom and Dad's silver anniversary!"

How could this date have snuck up so suddenly? Last year she, Elizabeth, and Steven had decided to do something big to commemorate Mom and Dad's big two-five. Nanny and Grandpa had even agreed to pay for the whole thing. But now it was less than a week away! Why wasn't anything in the works yet? Why hadn't Elizabeth been nagging at her every six seconds about not forgetting?

Jessica's face twisted into a scowl. She knew exactly why her twin hadn't been in major control-freak mode lately. She'd been lost on Planet Jeff for the past few weeks.

"Guess it's up to me to get things started," she mumbled.

Picking up her organizer, she walked down the hallway into Elizabeth's bedroom.

"Liz, look at this!" she said, holding open the book and pointing to the circled date. "We totally forgot about Mom and Dad's—" She broke off abruptly and looked around.

Was she even in the right room? She had noticed Elizabeth was getting a little bit sloppy lately, but *still*. Typically her twin's bedroom looked like something out of a furniture catalog. Her bed was always made, her things were always in place, and she could usually be found hunched over her desk, studying. This scene was more like Jessica's room—actually it would probably be clean by Jessica's standards, but *not* by Elizabeth's. The normal Elizabeth, that was.

Clothes and shoes were scattered about the floor. Her desk was buried under a lopsided pile of books and papers. And in the middle of her unmade bed lay Elizabeth, talking on the telephone. One leg was propped on the other and her long blond hair hung over the side of the mattress.

"Excuse me, Jeff," she said into the receiver, then she covered the mouthpiece with her hand and frowned at Jessica. "What is it, Jess? I'm kind of busy right now."

Jessica was about to say, "Doesn't look like it to me," but decided against it. Instead she held up the organizer and thumped the open page. "Next week is Mom and Dad's anniversary!" she said.

She braced herself for Elizabeth to begin freaking. Instead Elizabeth just let out an annoyed sigh. "Can't we talk about this later?" she asked. "I'm in the middle of a conversation."

Jessica's mouth dropped open. Had Jeffy-Poo completely warped Elizabeth's mind? Were all of her logical, responsible brain cells swimming in hormones?

"Fine," Jessica said. She snapped the organizer shut and headed out the door.

She'd been so ready to do something about this anniversary. Only now what? Was she supposed to wait until Elizabeth and Jeff were done whispering sweet nothings? *That* could take all night.

Suddenly she had an idea. Being a respectable college guy, Steven would definitely want to get things going. In fact, he might have already started planning the whole thing and just not filled them in yet.

She headed into her room and picked up her cordless. *Thank you, separate phone lines.* If it wasn't for that nifty luxury, no one else in the family would have a chance with the way Elizabeth and Jeff clocked in the talk time.

Sitting up against her headboard, she carefully punched Steven's number. After several rings there came a click, followed by a hurried-sounding "Hello?"

"Uh . . . Steven? It's Jessica."

"Hey, what's up, Space?"

Jessica cringed. She was really sick of these stupid nicknames he had for her. "I'm calling about Mom and Dad's big day. We *do* have something planned, right?"

"Huh? What big day?"

"Their anniversary," she said, rolling her eyes.

Silence.

"Their *twenty-fifth* anniversary?" she added. "Next Thursday?" Now who was the space case?

"Oh, yeah. Man, I totally forgot. No, we don't

have anything planned."

"Steven! We have less than a week."

"Yeah. I know. Look, can I call you back? I'm on the other line."

Jessica raised an eyebrow. "Heather?"

"Heather? Where have you been? It's Rachel now." His voice grew softer as he mentioned her name.

"Rachel?" Jessica repeated, wrinkling up her nose.

"Yeah. So . . . later, okay? Bye."

"Bye, Steven," she mumbled, but he had already hung up.

Jessica sighed and set the phone back on its base. Something really strange was going on around here. Since when did she become the only responsible Wakefield child?

Jessica Wakefield

Ideas for Mom and Dad's
Anniversary Celebration

— Book them a romantic horse-and-carriage ride?

No. Too bumpy for pouring champagne.

Besides, there's the whole smell issue.

— Rent them a private yacht for a one-night "love cruise"?

Nah. Mom tends to get seasick. In fact, she'd probably get seasick on a carriage ride.

— Hire musicians for a private at-home serenade?

Could be tough. Knowing Dad's taste in music, I'd probably have to exhume the musicians.

— Throw a party at the kiddie arcade like we did for Jeremy?

Cute, but I'm thinking no. If they can't figure out how to program the VCR, they'd probably be really lost on all the video games.

— Go completely retro and book the fancy ballroom at the top of the Hyatt?

All I can say is: Daddy trying to dance? Eeek! Run for the exits!

Oh, well. Maybe Liz will have better ideas.

Elizabeth Wakefield

Ideas for Mom and Dad's Anniversary Celebration

—Go on a carriage ride like Jeff took me on that time?

It might not be Mom and Dad's sort of thing, but we sure had fun. It was so cozy and romantic, and Jeff looked so amazing in the moonlight. . . .

Okay. What was I thinking about? Something about me and Jeff celebrating something?

CHAPTER *Whiplash* 3

Evan shifted from one foot to the other as he waited for someone to answer the Marsdens' front door. He really hoped Andy was home. He was going crazy by himself and just needed to hang with someone for a while. And maybe, if the opportunity came, he could get another perspective on the whole Berkeley thing.

The door opened, and Andy stood there, his green T-shirt covered with crumbs and his curly red hair sticking up in the back. "Hey!" he greeted him. "What are you doing here?"

Evan tilted his head. "Am I interrupting anything?"

Andy laughed. "Actually, I'm sort of embarrassed to tell you what I was doing."

"Try me."

"I was eating Pringles and watching a rerun of *SpongeBob SquarePants*."

Evan grinned. "You're useless as a human being. You know that, right?"

"Hey, we can't all save the world." Andy pushed

open the door and beckoned Evan inside. "You want to go down to the game room and shoot some pool?"

"Sounds cool."

He followed Andy down the carpeted staircase and into the giant, wood-paneled game room. While Andy racked the billiard balls, Evan stared out the window at the large, kidney-shaped swimming pool shimmering in the sunlight outside. He already felt a little better. Andy's place had a way of relaxing him. Maybe it was because the Marsden house was so centered around fun and relaxation with its game room, swimming pool, video games, and wide-screen TV. His own house was nice, just not as . . . recreational.

"So how come you aren't with Jade?" Andy asked as he sorted the balls inside the large plastic triangle.

"She and her mom are out having a late dinner," Evan explained. "Apparently they need some quality time."

"Ah, quality time. Well, I'm flattered you thought of me." Andy handed Evan a pool cue. "You want to break?"

"Sure." Evan grabbed the stick, lined up his trajectory, and shot. The cue ball hit with a high-pitched *thwack*, sending balls scurrying in every direction. He immediately sank the four and the six, and the two ball stopped short of a side pocket. Evan walked around the table and finished off the two.

For a while they played and said nothing other than the occasional "nice shot." Evan liked that about Andy. In a crowd he talked nonstop—especially if he was nervous. But one-on-one he seemed to know the value of comfortable silence, and he could always sense when Evan was in a mood to talk and when he wasn't.

"Eight ball in the corner pocket," Evan said. He made a clean, swift stroke with the cue and the black ball disappeared.

"Good game," Andy remarked.

Out of years of habit, Evan immediately began racking up the balls for another game.

"So did you find out anything more about this Berkeley thing?" Andy asked.

Evan sighed and slouched against the stereo cabinet. "Sort of," he replied. "I saw Mr. Nelson today."

"Ah. What did ol' Furry Face have to say?"

Evan paused. Andy knew Tia better than almost anyone. So much depended on how he reacted to this. "He said my best chance would be if one of the three Sweet Valley students who got in turned Berkeley down." He finished racking and stepped back to let Andy break.

Andy paused while lining up his shot. He looked right at Evan. "Really? That's what he said?"

"Yep."

"Huh. Interesting." Andy took the shot and split

41

the pack of billiard balls. Then he reached for a cube of chalk and began twisting it over the tip of his cue.

"So Jade had a strange idea," Evan went on, tossing his stick from one hand to the other.

"What's that?" Andy asked, sinking the ten ball.

"She said I should basically ask Tia for her spot." Evan felt his heartbeat accelerate.

Andy stood up straight and began chalking his stick again. He started to nod. "You know, that's a great idea," he said.

"Really?" Evan felt like he was filling with helium. "You think so?"

"Sure. I mean, I don't think Tia's all that hot on Berkeley anyway. And she'd probably get a kick out of helping you." He looked at Evan and grinned. "I say go for it."

Evan felt his face crack into a wide smile. Why had he been so worried? Of course he could approach Tia about Berkeley. And once Tia turned Berkeley down, his chances would improve immensely. It still wouldn't be a sure thing, but it was odds he could live with.

He wanted to kiss Jade for her brilliant plan. He could even kiss Andy! Then again, he'd probably just kiss Jade twice.

"Thanks, man," Evan said, giving Andy a playful shove with the thick end of his pool stick. "I mean it. Thanks a lot. I should go right home and call Tia."

"Hey. Wait a sec. We've got to finish the game first. You at least owe me that." He looked at Evan and raised his eyebrows in mock seriousness. "Come on, man. SpongeBob SquarePants wouldn't leave a game undone."

"Fine, fine," Evan said, stepping up to the table. He had no idea whose turn it was. He couldn't even remember if he was stripes or solids. All he wanted to do was talk to Tia and worm his way into Berkeley.

Then he could get started on the rest of his life.

"Could you believe the way Melissa smirked all through practice?" Cherie said. "I mean, does she not realize she isn't Empress of the World anymore?"

"What I want to know is how you managed to hold her up when we did the pyramid," Amy chimed in, pointing a french fry at Gina.

"Tell me about it," Gina said, rolling her eyes. "I wanted so bad to shrug and send her flying."

"Ooh. I'll give you fifty dollars if you do that next practice," Lila said, raising an eyebrow. The other girls laughed.

Will leaned against the vinyl-covered table at First and Ten. His temples throbbed, and his body felt exhausted.

Maybe this was a mistake. Maybe he shouldn't have joined up with the gang. He wasn't exactly in a social mood, but when the guys brought it up, he'd figured it would beat sitting around at home, feeling cruddy. He'd hoped it would be cool and laid-back. Instead it ended up being a big Melissa slam. It always amazed him how quickly and completely girls could turn on each other.

Not that he didn't think she deserved it. After what she pulled, he should jump right in and skewer her along with everyone else. It was just that Melissa was the last thing he wanted to think or talk about right now.

Josh nudged him in the ribs. "So has she been calling you to beg forgiveness?" he asked.

"No way, man," Will replied. "Even if she did, I wouldn't listen."

"Oh, I'm sure she'll call," Gina remarked. "She'll probably be all melodramatic and threaten to swallow a bottle of pills or something."

The others laughed, but Will felt the blood drain out of his face. *That* wasn't funny. The last time Melissa had pulled a crazy stunt like that had been the worst thing he'd ever gone through. He really hoped she wasn't stupid enough to try it again.

Cherie shook her head. "No, she won't do that old routine again. Remember what she said in the locker room?" Cherie's green eyes grew wide. "She's going to become a serious East Coast college girl now."

The girls dissolved into giggles.

Will sat forward. "She what?"

"Melissa's been accepted to Smith College," Amy explained. "Her *'dream school.'*"

Will felt a strange thud inside his chest. Melissa was going to Smith? When did that happen? And when had she been planning to tell him all this? Not that it mattered now. But still. If this had been in the works all along, did it mean she'd never planned on being with him after graduation?

"Where's Smith College?" Matt asked through a mouthful of burger.

"In Massachusetts," Gina answered. "And get this . . . it's an *all-girl school!*"

"Whoa," Josh exclaimed.

"What I want to know," Cherie began, turning her head to meet everyone's gaze, "is how does she plan on surviving this place if there are no guys around to manipulate? She won't last a week!"

Aaron threw back his head and laughed. A little too loudly, Will thought. He knew Aaron was just trying to cover up his embarrassment at having been played by Melissa—and he was probably trying to get back in good with Cherie. But it still bugged him.

In fact, it really wasn't Aaron he was mad at. Or any of the people sitting here. It was Melissa. For years they had talked about going off to the same college. They'd planned to stay in dorms the first couple of years and then maybe rent a place together—if they could get her parents to agree to it. They'd even talked about getting a pet. He wanted a dog, but she always insisted on a cat—a black one that she would call Sadie. Now all of a sudden it was off to Massachusetts? Everything had gotten so different so fast, he couldn't help but feel a little whiplash.

Get over it, he told himself. *Obviously Liss is moving on. Why can't you?*

Suddenly Will remembered something—the letter from NYU. He *was* moving on. All the way to the Big Apple, in fact. He smiled. Then he sat forward and cleared his throat. "Hey, guys. Speaking of college, I've got some news."

"What?" Josh asked. The others grew silent and stared at him expectantly.

Will took a deep breath and said, "I got accepted to New York University."

"Hey, cool." Aaron raised his hand and high-fived Will. Matt and Josh followed suit.

"Oh my God, Will!" Cherie screeched. "That's awesome!"

Suddenly he found himself being hugged and patted by all the girls. If Melissa thought she could just run off to an East Coast school and totally blow off everything, fine. She wasn't the only one.

*   *   *

46

"Well, here we are," Jeff declared as he and Elizabeth stepped onto the Wakefields' front porch and faced each other.

Elizabeth smiled. It was funny how Jeff always said "here we are" at the end of the date, as if it had been their main destination all along. In fact, it was the part she liked the least. Especially tonight.

"I'm sorry," she said for about the twenty-second time that night. "I really wish we could stay out later."

Jeff placed his hands around her waist and pulled her close. "It's all right," he said. "It's not your fault the *Scope* has a major deadline tomorrow. Besides, the fact that they want you there early to help them out is proof of how much they rely on you."

How awesome was this guy?

Jeff leaned forward and gave her a long, lingering kiss. "Good night, Liz," he murmured, his breath against her neck. Her skin went all tingly, as always.

"Good night," she said. They let go of each other and Jeff stepped off the porch backward, lifting his hand in a small wave.

The phone was ringing as she walked inside, jolting her out of the nice peaceful state Jeff had left her in. She ran into the living room and snatched up the receiver. "Hello?"

"Hey, Brain. Where's Airhead?"

"Steven?" Elizabeth's brow furrowed. Why was

her brother calling on a Friday night? "Um, Jessica's working tonight. Why?"

"I was supposed to call her back. She called me up all freaked out about this anniversary thing for Mom and Dad."

"Oh, yeah," Elizabeth said, remembering. She sat down on the sofa and kicked off her shoes. "She ran into my room screaming about it too."

"So what have you got planned?"

Elizabeth frowned. Why did everyone assume she would tackle the project herself? Didn't they know how busy she was? "Nothing, Steven. I haven't had a chance."

"Uh . . . okay. Don't you think we should get something going soon? I mean, we don't have much time."

"Yeah, sure. Let's just book a restaurant somewhere." It really bugged her that everyone seemed to think this was automatically her responsibility. Weren't there two other siblings in the family?

"Actually, it *is* a big deal, isn't it?" Steven countered. "I mean, they have been married for twenty-five years now. But whatever. Any ideas for the restaurant?"

Elizabeth shut her eyes. She tried to think of a nice, fancy place, but for some reason, all she could think of was Jeff. His eyes. His kisses. The way he held her on the porch. She wondered what he could be planning for tomorrow—he'd told her he was taking her on a surprise mystery date.

48

Suddenly she remembered something he once told her—about a restaurant his parents really loved. "How about Saki?" she said. "You know, that cool, Cal-sushi place everyone's raving about?"

"Sounds good to me," Steven replied. "I guess we should check it out first, though. You want to meet there tomorrow evening and see if we can reserve a section?"

Elizabeth shook her head. "Can't. I'm busy. But I know Jess isn't working, and Jeremy is—so she's probably free. I'll let her know."

Steven sighed. "Are you sure you can't make it?"

"Positive. I've got something really important." Elizabeth smiled to herself.

"Okay. Tell Jess to be there at six o'clock *on the dot*. I've got stuff to do too."

"No problem. Bye, Steven." She hung up and flopped back against the couch cushions.

"Hello?" came Andy's sleepy-sounding voice.

"Hey. I'm bored."

"Um . . . and who might this be?"

"Come on, Andy. You know it's me. I just wanted to talk awhile." Tia rolled over on her back. "I'm sooooo bored."

"Why do people always think of me when they've got nothing to do?" Andy demanded. "Do they automatically assume I have a blank social calendar?"

"Do you have anything on your calendar tonight?"

"No, I'm bored," Andy replied, exhaling heavily. "Dave went with his dad to check out some college."

"College. *Ugh!*" Tia groaned. "I'm so sick of that subject. All anyone can ask these days is, 'Where are you going?' 'Have you made up your mind yet?' It's such a pain!"

"Believe me, I know. It certainly seems to be the theme of the evening anyway."

Tia's brow furrowed. "What do you mean?"

"Evan just left a little while ago. Jade was busy, and he also needed some cheering up."

"He's still stressing over Berkeley, isn't he?" Tia shook her head. "That's so weird they turned him down. He must be majorly bummed. I wish I could say something to cheer him up."

There came a short pause. Then Andy gave a quick laugh and said, "You know something, Tia? You *can*."

Call Tia. Call Tia. Call Tia.
The thought provided a simple rhythm as Evan strode up the sidewalk and then through his front door. He couldn't wait to call Tia and ask her about giving up the spot. Jade had been right about it making perfect sense. After talking to Andy, he knew he had to go for it. After all, Andy knew Tia better than practically anybody.

50

If he said it was a good idea, then it must be a good idea.

As Evan ran into the house, he could hear the phone ringing in the kitchen. Probably Jade checking up on him. He *had* been a real pain lately. But just wait until she heard what Andy said.

Evan snatched the receiver off the wall. "Hello?"

"Um, Evan?"

"Andy?" Evan blinked. "Didn't I just leave you, like, a few minutes ago?"

"Yeah. Listen, I've got to tell you something really impor—"

The call waiting beeped, cutting off the end of Andy's sentence. *That* was probably Jade.

"Just a sec, Andy. Let me get that."

He pressed the flash button.

"Hello, Plummer residence," Evan said jokingly. He hadn't felt this good in a while.

"Evan?" came a familiar female voice—only it wasn't Jade.

"Tia? Wow, Tee, what a coincidence. I was just going to call—"

"Were you seriously going to ask me to do that?" she interrupted.

"Huh?"

"I just talked to Andy, and he told me that you were thinking of asking me to turn down Berkeley just on the *hopes* that it would improve your chance.

51

But you're not actually serious about that, right?"

Evan felt his whole body sag. Jade had been wrong. Andy had been wrong. This didn't look good at all. "No, Andy's right," he said.

"I can't believe you, Evan. I mean, don't you see how out of line that is? You think you can just ask for my Berkeley spot and I'm supposed to hand it over like it's no big deal?"

"Uh . . . no." He shook his head. "I mean, not like that. I just thought—"

"You know you're my friend, and I feel terrible that you didn't get in. But you're putting me in a really bad position. I might be a little mixed up about where to go and whether I want to go straight to college, but that doesn't give you the right to assume I won't mind just giving up a great opportunity."

Evan sat down in one of the kitchen chairs, his energy completely sapped. There was no point in trying to defend himself—she was obviously not going to listen.

"Yeah, okay, I don't know if Berkeley's right for me yet. But there are plenty of good reasons why it could be."

"Really?" Evan said, his temper flaring. "And what are those good reasons, Tia? Just how much do you even *know* about the college I've dreamed of going to for as long as I can remember?"

For the first time since the conversation started, Tia was silent.

"Tia?" Evan prodded.

"I'm sorry, Evan, but you're just asking too much," she said. She muttered a quick good-bye and hung up. For several seconds he just sat there, listening to the empty nothing at the other end of the line. Then he slowly stood and replaced the receiver on its base.

Immediately it started to ring again. He'd totally forgotten Andy on the other line.

"Hey," he greeted, picking the phone back up.

"Evan!" Andy screeched. "Listen, whatever you do, *don't* call Tia. She called right after you left, and I sort of told her what you were planning, and she freaked out. So you might want to steer clear of her right now, okay?"

"Thanks, Andy," Evan mumbled. "But you're too late. That was her on the other line."

"Oh."

"But hey. Thanks for trying," Evan said.

"Listen. You still have a chance. I bet you could still get in without her help."

"Thanks. See ya, Andy." Evan hung up and stood facing the kitchen wall. Andy was wrong. He had no chance at Berkeley. Obviously the only chance he'd had just blew up in his face.

TIA RAMIREZ

WHEN YOU COME FROM A LARGE FAMILY, YOU HAVE TO GET USED TO SHARING THINGS. IT'S LIKE SOME UNWRITTEN LAW OF PHYSICS. YOU CAN CARVE YOUR NAME INTO SOMETHING, CHAIN IT TO YOUR ANKLE, SURROUND IT WITH BARBED WIRE, AND BROTHERS AND SISTERS WILL <u>STILL</u> MANAGE TO GET HOLD OF IT. THE TERM <u>PERSONAL PROPERTY</u> MEANS NOTHING WHEN YOU HAVE SIBLINGS.

TAKE MY BROTHERS (<u>PLEASE!</u>). THEY ARE ALWAYS GETTING INTO MY STUFF. WHEN I WAS TEN, MY BROTHER JESSE "BORROWED" MY BICYCLE AND ENTERED A RAMP-JUMPING CONTEST. HE DID FINALLY RETURN IT TO ME—WITH A BENT FRAME. EVEN NOW HE AND MY OTHER BROTHERS ARE ALWAYS

USING MY COMPUTER. AND I CAN'T EVEN COUNT THE NUMBER OF PAPERBACKS, SUNGLASSES, PACKS OF CHEWING GUM, AND LOOSE CHANGE THAT HAVE MYSTERIOUSLY DISAPPEARED FROM MY BEDROOM, NEVER TO BE SEEN AGAIN. AS YOU MIGHT GUESS, DEFINING WHAT'S MINE IN THE WORLD HAS BEEN AN ONGOING BATTLE.

BUT IT'S NOT JUST MY BROTHERS EITHER. FOR A LONG TIME I THOUGHT ANGEL WAS ALL MINE. HE WASN'T. GAMBLING TOOK HIM AWAY FOR A WHILE. THEN STANFORD. NOW HE'S WITH SOMEONE ELSE. WE'RE SUPPOSEDLY STILL FRIENDS, BUT I BARELY HEAR FROM HIM.

NOT THAT YOU CAN EVER LAY CLAIM TO YOUR FRIENDS EITHER. I HAD TO LEARN TO SHARE

CONNER WITH LIZ, THEN ALANNA.
AND IT'S STRANGE NOT TO HAVE
ANDY CONSTANTLY AVAILABLE
FOR SOME TALK TIME. SINCE HE
AND DAVE HOOKED UP, HE
HARDLY EVER COMES AROUND.

ANYWAY. I GUESS WHAT I'M
TRYING TO SAY IS THAT THE
BERKELEY SPOT HAS BEEN ONE
OF THE FEW THINGS I'VE GOTTEN
THAT IS TOTALLY AND COMPLETELY
MINE. IT'S MINE TO ACCEPT OR
TURN DOWN—BUT IT'S <u>MINE.</u> SO
WHAT IF I'M NOT AS IN LOVE WITH
THE SCHOOL AS EVAN IS? THAT
DOESN'T MEAN HE HAS A RIGHT
TO TAKE IT AWAY, DOES IT?
ESPECIALLY WHEN THERE'S NO
GUARANTEE IT WOULD EVEN GO
TO HIM.

UNTIL I KNOW FOR SURE WHAT
I WANT TO DO WITH MY FUTURE,
I'M HOLDING ON TO THAT SPOT

WITH BOTH HANDS. I'VE LEARNED
THE HARD WAY THAT IF YOU LET
SOMETHING OUT OF YOUR SIGHT,
YOU CAN LOSE IT FOREVER. SO
FORGIVE ME IF I DON'T FEEL ALL
SHARE HAPPY RIGHT NOW.

CHAPTER 4
Giving a Plastic Bear the Evil Eye

"Saturday. Goody," Evan muttered sarcastically as he trudged into the kitchen. He was still pretty tired since he'd barely slept last night, but he just couldn't bear lying in bed frowning up at the ceiling fan anymore. Maybe some strong herbal tea or union-grown coffee would snap him out of his funk.

Yeah, right, he thought. He doubted any drink out there could bring him out of this self-pity fest. After his conversation with Tia he'd tried his hardest to force all thoughts of Berkeley from his mind. But they always crept back in when he let his guard down. Eventually he gave up and let himself wallow in his misery.

"I've got to get a grip," he mumbled.

Evan limped over to the pantry and took out a box of Morning Thunder tea bags and a bottle of honey. He set the items on the counter and reached for the teakettle. Suddenly he froze and turned back again, staring at the honey container. It was a small plastic bottle in the shape of a smiling bear. *Bears,* his brain processed wearily. *The Berkeley Bears*. Yet another reminder of his loss.

There was no escape. Anytime he tried to focus on other things, something would trigger thoughts of Berkeley. And every little reminder hit him like a slap in the face.

He'd never realized before how everything in his life seemed to hinge on his getting into Berkeley. He'd always imagined himself heading up some politically active organization someday after he'd graduated *from Berkeley*. Or taking a year or two off *from Berkeley* to serve in the Peace Corps. Or starting up a new radical magazine with his *compadres at Berkeley*. Since that part of his future would never happen, he wasn't sure how to plot the rest of it. It was like using a compass with no needle.

Evan blinked a couple of times and shook his head. What was he doing? Was he actually standing in the middle of his kitchen, giving a plastic bear the evil eye?

He grabbed the teakettle and headed to the sink. As he filled the round metal basin with water, he reached down with his free hand and tossed a couple of cool splashes onto his face. He had to find a way to deal with this—and soon. If he didn't get a handle on it now, he could see himself, years later, leading a seemingly normal life except for the spastic fits of rage he'd fly into whenever anyone mentioned Berkeley.

As he set the kettle on the stove and fired up the

burner, he could hear someone whistling on the stoop outside. The cheerful-sounding noise made him feel even more morose in comparison. The lid of the brass mailbox clanged shut, and the whistling grew fainter.

Might as well make myself useful and bring in the mail, he thought. He opened the door and stepped outside, his mouth gaping into a wide yawn.

The concrete of the porch was cool against his bare feet. Hopping from one leg to the other, he reached into the mailbox and found one lonely post-card. Hardly worth the effort. But at least some trees had been spared.

He spun around to head inside, flipping the card over in his hand. Suddenly he stopped, his body growing numb. Stamped on the front of the card was the familiar Berkeley logo. Evan turned the card around and read:

> *Dear Prospective Student:*
>
> *You are cordially invited to join fellow Berkeley applicants in your area for our Spring University Symposium. Come meet representatives from every department, check out our wide range of clubs and organizations, and talk with student advisers. See for yourself why the University of California at Berkeley continues to be one of the country's best schools.*

Evan sighed, his breath forming a small cloud of vapor that lingered in the air a few seconds before dispersing. *At least they think enough of me to invite me to this thing,* he thought. *That's* something.

He slid his finger down the card, checking the date. It was going to be this Wednesday evening at the nearby civic center. The list of featured clubs and speakers was amazing. He could spend the entire night there and still not see everything he wanted.

Of course, he should probably just stay home. If he went, he might get even more fired up about the school. That would make it hurt worse if he didn't get in. And it hurt badly enough already.

Then again, if he went, he might discover another way of improving his chances. Maybe he could make some crucial connections. Or maybe if they met him in person and heard what he had to say, they'd automatically bump him up a few places. It was worth a shot.

Evan went back inside and pinned the postcard to the bulletin board near the door. He could feel a tiny spot of warmth well up inside him, like a small surge of power. Maybe he'd even try whistling. In fact, he could almost hear a whistle in his head right now. Sort of a high-pitched shriek.

Oh, wait. That was the teakettle.

*   *   *

Jessica padded around her bedroom in her bare feet Saturday night, picking things off her shelves and studying them as if browsing in a gift shop. Just her luck, she'd had to work at House of Java last night, and Jeremy had to work tonight. So much for having quality time with her boyfriend this weekend.

She had hoped to talk Elizabeth into a girls' night since she hadn't seen much of her lately. She'd pictured them running out for videos and gourmet ice cream, maybe even discussing their parents' anniversary party a bit before starting up their own fun. Unfortunately her sister didn't even have time to say two words to her when she got back from the *Scope* that afternoon. Just showered, dressed, primped, and shot out of the house like a cannonball when Jeff rang the doorbell. Now there was nothing left but lame TV reruns for company.

"Who needs Liz?" Jessica muttered. She flopped backward on her bed, lifted her legs, and tried to balance a stuffed rabbit on her feet. "In fact, who needs anybody? I'll just treat this as a night to relax."

She smiled. Actually, that was a great idea. She could give herself a mini–spa treatment at home. Jessica grabbed her rabbit, sat back up, and stared into his glassy black eyes. "We don't need a date tonight, do we? We just need a little pampering."

A few minutes later she was dressed in her fluffy

bathrobe and lying against the feather pillows on her bed, a deep-pore clay mask drying on her face. A soothing Sarah McLachlan CD was on the stereo, and the overhead light was off. Her bedside lamp provided just enough light for her to paint her nails Saucy Lilac.

"What do you think?" she asked her bunny, who lay on his side next to her. She wiggled her left fingers in front of his whiskers. "Think they need another coat?" The bunny stared back at her blankly.

Jessica sighed. *This is ridiculous,* she thought. Her face itched like crazy, but scratching it would not only mess up her facial, it would botch her nail polish too. She gazed at the starlight peeping through the gap in her window curtains. She could almost feel the fun and excitement going on other places—without her.

Scooting down against her pillows, she yawned as much as her tight mask would allow. At least her skin would look great tomorrow . . .

Jessica started drifting off to sleep. A dream began, with Jeremy handing her a bouquet of saucy lilacs. Suddenly a shrill sound cut through her thoughts. She sat up abruptly, Jeremy's image vanishing before her eyes, and glanced around for the source of the noise. The phone was ringing.

Maybe it's Jeremy calling from work, she thought hopefully. Careful not to smudge her new manicure, she reached for the phone.

"Hello?" she murmured sleepily.

"Jessica?"

"Steven?" So her brother had finally decided to call her back—a whole day late. "Hey. What's up?"

"What's up?" he repeated, his voice an angry hiss. "What are *you* doing?"

Jessica's tight brow wrinkled. "Giving myself a facial?" she replied.

Steven let out a loud, aggravated grunt. "I don't believe it. That is so typical. I've been waiting around here for an hour and a half and you're back home playing beauty parlor!"

"Hey!" Jessica protested. "I don't know what you're talking about. I should be yelling at you. You're the one who never called me back last night."

"What is this? Revenge? For your information I *did* call back and talked to Liz instead. And it's a good thing too since you obviously can't be counted on!"

Jessica moved the receiver away from her ear as Steven's voice continued to rise. "So you talked to Liz, huh?" she said during a pause. She nodded slowly to herself. Suddenly it was all starting to make sense.

"That's right. So *if* you can drag yourself away from your mirror, tell our sister that I *tried* to book the restaurant but that *someone* didn't show up to help me check it out," Steven spat across the phone line. Then he hung up.

Jessica could hear a quick series of clicks, followed by the dial tone. Obviously Elizabeth had spaced out and forgotten to fill her in on some plans she made with Steven. Classic. Lately she'd been too busy swooning over Jeff to even say hi. Taking the time to pass along some important details must have been too tall an order.

So now Steven thought Jessica was the ditz. Steven was mad at *her*, when it was Elizabeth he should be yelling at.

Jessica whacked the pillow beside her with her elbow. She was sick of Elizabeth blowing everything off for her boyfriend. As soon as she got back from her date, Jessica was going to confront her. She'd really let her have it. In fact, she was going to lie back and rehearse every single thing she would say.

Of course, she probably should turn the Sarah McLachlan CD off first. It always made her so sleepy. . . .

Elizabeth sat up in bed Sunday morning, stretching her arms. Sunlight was streaming through her window, filling her bedroom with a golden glow. She sighed dreamily and sank back against her pillows. Last night with Jeff had been hands down the most romantic night of her life. She wished she could go right back to sleep and replay the whole evening like a movie.

He had taken her to—of all places—an ice-skating rink. He had a good friend who was comanager of The Great Ice-Cape, and the guy actually closed the place for a half hour so they could be alone.

Afterward they went to a café near the beach and had hot cocoa. Everything was so warm and cozy. She hadn't felt that snug since she was little.

The phone started ringing beside her. *How sweet,* she thought. *Jeff wants to be the first voice I hear today.*

"Hello-o," she sang into the receiver. She scooped up a pillow with her free hand and hugged it as if Jeff were right there with her.

"Um, Elizabeth? Is that you?"

Elizabeth frowned. "Evan?"

"Yeah. Listen, I'm sorry to call so early. I just really needed to talk to someone."

"Sounds major," she said. "What's wrong?"

"I don't know if you heard or not, but Berkeley rejected me."

Elizabeth winced. "Oh, Evan. That's awful."

She heard him sigh. "Yeah. It's really driving me nuts. I can't sleep. I can't eat. I really thought I had it made. Now everything's changed—everything."

Elizabeth's heart tugged. She'd never heard Evan sound so down. "What do your parents say?" she asked.

"I haven't told them yet," he replied. "I guess I

don't want them to throw a bunch of advice at me. That's the thing. No one's just *listening* to me. Jade's so angry at Berkeley, she almost seems more upset than me. Mr. Nelson says I should apply somewhere else and move on. Tia and Andy . . ." His voice trailed off.

"Hey," Elizabeth said sympathetically. "I'm here. You know I'll listen to you."

At that moment Elizabeth's bedroom door banged opened and Jessica came storming in. At least, it had to be Jessica. Whoever it was wore a bathrobe similar to her sister's, but her hair stood out in all directions and crusty gray globs stuck to her face. Her eyes flashed with anger as she marched up to the side of the bed.

"You have some real explaining to do!" she shrieked.

Elizabeth just blinked in confusion.

"Liz? Is everything okay?" Evan asked.

"Um—hold on a sec," she said into the phone. "Jessica? Could you come back later? This is sort of important."

"I bet it is!" Jessica yelled. "Tell Jeff you'll make kissy noises with him some other time. We need to talk!"

Elizabeth rolled her eyes. Her sister could be so dramatic sometimes. "This isn't Jeff. It's Evan, and *he* really needs to talk."

Jessica's blue-green eyes grew wide, and tiny gray flakes shot off her skin. "Well, so do I!"

"Fine," Elizabeth replied. Obviously Jessica wasn't

going to give on this one. She probably just wanted to lecture Elizabeth about borrowing her special French hand cream. "Hey, Evan. I'm sorry, but I really need to call you back," she mumbled into the phone.

"Uh . . . okay. Sure," he replied. "Later."

Elizabeth felt terrible. She had just promised to listen to him as a good, loyal friend, then two seconds later she blew him off. She shook her head as she hung up the phone. "Okay," she said to Jessica. "This better be good."

Jessica raised her chin defiantly. "Steven called last night," she said.

"Yeah? So?"

Jessica scowled, causing another avalanche of gray flakes. "*So* he was wondering where I was! Apparently he'd been waiting somewhere for me for an hour and a half, only I never showed up. Know why? *Because I had no idea I was supposed to be there!*"

Elizabeth cringed. Okay, her sister did have a right to be annoyed—though it wasn't exactly a major tragedy. How many times had Jessica flaked on delivering a message? "I'm sorry, Jess. I was superbusy yesterday, and I forgot to tell you to meet him at Saki. Jeff's parents love that place, and I thought we could book it for Mom and Dad's anniversary party."

Jessica exhaled sharply and crossed her arms over her chest. "First of all, what do you mean you 'forgot'?

This is important. And second . . . *duh*. Haven't you forgotten something else? Like, that Mom absolutely hates sushi?"

Elizabeth bit her lip. How did *that* slip her mind? She really must be overworked lately.

"Liz! We only have four days to plan this," Jessica whined. "You're never available, and now Steven thinks I ditched him when it was really your fault. Come on. I could really use a reliable sister here. Think you could snap out of your lovesick Jeff daze long enough to help me on this?"

"Okay, okay." Elizabeth waved a hand in surrender. Her twin could really lay on the hysterics sometimes. "Look, I'll call Steven and straighten things out. As far as the anniversary, why don't we meet at Le Chateau tomorrow after your cheerleading practice and my *Oracle* meeting? We know they love that place."

Jessica nodded. "All right," she said finally. "Fine." She turned and headed toward the door. As she was about to step into the hallway, she leaned her head back and said, "You sure you won't forget?"

"Jess!" Elizabeth exclaimed. "Of course I won't forget!"

"Good," Jessica replied, and disappeared down the hall.

To: mcdermott@cal.rr.com
From: marsden1@swiftnet.com
Subject: re: Big Gig

   Hey. Got your message about the gig. I'd come, but I think I might have a gig myself that night at a new comedy club. Gotta go please the fans and catch all the underwear women throw at me. You know how it is.
   Have you told Evan yet? He'd probably be up for it. The guy needs a major mood lifter. If you haven't heard, he got turned down by Berkeley. And Tia got in. It's a long story, but whatever you do, DON'T mention Berkeley around him or Tia. Consider yourself warned.

                   —Andy

Will Simmons

Reasons Why I Shouldn't Fill Out and Mail the NYU Acceptance Letter Yet

I've had tons of homework, and my wrist feels sort of cramped from writing so much. I don't want to cause a serious injury that might affect my ability to do well in college.

I should really make sure I have a good block of time to do the letter. Sometime when I won't have any interruptions. I'm just too swamped to schedule it this week.

I really should double-check some of the information I need to include.

Like my full name and Social Security Number. For all I know, I've had it wrong these past several years.

A delay could be good. I really don't want to look too eager, right?

There's a full moon coming up these next couple of days. Isn't it bad luck to send a letter during a full moon?

CHAPTER
PICK-ON-TIA DAY
5

"Have you ever noticed that you can tell what grade someone's in just by watching them walk down the hall?" Andy asked. He pointed his onion ring toward the nearby empty hallway.

Evan frowned. He'd spent all day yesterday freaking out over the whole Berkeley situation. Then he'd hardly slept last night. All he could focus on right now was his soggy cafeteria salad and lukewarm bottled water—he wasn't up for Andy's jokes.

But Andy didn't even wait for a response. "I mean, take the freshmen, for instance. You always see them carrying a mountain of textbooks and racing as fast as they can to their next class. Have they never heard of lockers? And what's with the fear on their faces? It's been a while, so I can't really remember— were we tortured in junior high for being late?"

"I don't know," Evan said.

"Now, the seniors are like the total opposites," Andy went on. He leaned back in his seat to make room for his hand gestures. "They just sort of walk along with their friends, making their own little phalanx."

"*Phalanx?*" Evan repeated.

"Yeah. You know, when people line up and form a moving, human wall," Andy explained. "It was how they did battle in ancient Greece."

"Ancient Greece?"

Andy shrugged. "Hey, it's on that Nintendo game Olympiad."

"Whatever you say."

"Anyway." Andy cleared his throat and raised his hands to continue. "The seniors just mosey along in their *human walls*, oblivious to the warning bells and all the freshmen having to climb over them and squeeze between their legs."

Evan chuckled. "What about the sophomores and juniors?"

"They're sort of in between. They hang out in little gossip groups at their lockers and then take off like rockets when the warning bell sounds."

"Ah. I see." Evan nodded. "So is all this for a new routine or something?"

Andy grinned. "Maybe. I've got this gig at a new comedy club in the Valley on Wednesday night. Hey, you want to come? I promise I won't say phalanx."

"I don't know. . . ." At the mention of Wednesday, Evan's stress levels amplified. "See, there's this Berkeley thing that night. I keep thinking I should go, but I'm not sure. I mean, what if it just makes me more depressed?"

Andy's face scrunched into an apologetic expression. "Sorry, man. I can't take sides on this."

Take sides? What did he mean by that? It wasn't like Evan was asking him to do anything. He was just trying to vent to a friend.

Andy must be backing Tia on this, Evan realized. His stomach clenched. He hoped this didn't end up being a side-taking situation. He really didn't have the strength for a battle. Besides, it wouldn't exactly be fair since Tia was already the victor. She had the Berkeley spot.

"Hey, Ev?" Andy said.

"Yeah?" Evan glanced at him, hopeful. Maybe Andy really did understand. Maybe he could open up to him after all.

"Have you ever noticed the doors in the hallways have the hinges on the wrong side? I mean, one minute you're walking along, minding your own business, when *wham!* A big slab of oak flies out in front of you. I really think they should make crash helmets mandatory dress code."

"La plume est sur la table," Madame Dalton chanted, the beads on her bracelets rattling as she waved her hands like a conductor.

"La plume est sur la table," the class repeated.

"Très bien!" She raised her arms to signal another sentence. *"Le chat est noir."*

"Le chat est noir."

Tia yawned. What good was this class anyway? Who walked around saying things like, "Hello. My cat is black"? Either the people in France were extremely dull, or Madame Dalton was keeping all the good vocabulary from them.

"Oui. Très bien, classe." Madame Dalton applauded softly.

Tia tapped her pen against her desk and gazed out the window. One of these days she would really like to go to France. Paris, especially. She imagined herself sipping coffee at a sidewalk bistro, looking out at the Eiffel Tower. Of course, should anyone want to talk to her, she'd only be able to converse about the weather or describe her pets in wonderful detail. So she probably wouldn't be making many friends.

Suddenly the bell rang, snapping Tia from her thoughts.

"Bien, classe. C'est tout pour c'est jour." Madame Dalton stepped to the side and gestured toward the blackboard like a middle-aged Vanna White. *"Voilà! Le devoir."*

"Page eighty-five, questions one through forty,"

Tia said aloud as she started to scrawl the assignment in her notebook. But midway through, her pen stopped working. "Great," she muttered. She looked up and saw Jade passing by her desk.

"Hey, Jade."

Jade stopped and glanced down at her. "Yeah?"

Tia sighed in relief. "My pen chose this moment to tap out on me." She held up her empty blue ball-point. "Could I borrow yours for a sec so I can write down the assignment?"

"Gee, Tia. I don't think so," Jade replied, her mouth lifting in a wide, phony smile. "You see, it's *mine*. But I'll add your name to the waiting list." She threw her faux tiger-skin bag over her shoulder and strolled out the door.

Tia gaped after her. How mature was that?

"Whatever," Tia mumbled. She pulled a brown eyeliner pencil out of her purse and finished writing down the assignment. Then she quickly loaded her backpack and walked out into the hall.

Even though Elizabeth had been one of the first people out the door, she hadn't made it too far down the hallway. She was wandering along, apparently lost in some daydream. Tia easily caught up.

"Hey, Liz," she said, tapping her friend's shoulder.

Elizabeth whirled around. "Oh. Hey, Tia."

Tia chuckled. Did Elizabeth even realize she was

at school? "Where were you just now?" Tia asked. "With Jeff?"

Elizabeth's face flushed. "Yeah, sort of. Let's just say I had one of the best weekends of my life."

"You've got it bad," Tia murmured, shaking her head. She couldn't remember seeing Elizabeth this happy before. Even when she was dating Conner, there always seemed to be an underlying tension. But this? This looked like bliss.

"So, how are you and Trent?" Elizabeth asked. Tia could tell she was trying hard to seem interested, but her voice still sounded distracted, as if she was eager to go back to her daydream.

"We're good," Tia replied with a grin.

"Got any big romantic dates planned?"

Tia snorted. "If by 'romantic date' you mean sharing a bag of potato chips and watching a video at his place, then yes. We're supposed to get together Wednesday. Only"—she paused, scrunching up her nose—"I might have to call it off."

"Why?" Elizabeth asked.

Tia shrugged. "It's just that I got a postcard from Berkeley inviting me to this big symposium thing. I don't know. I don't really feel like going, but I guess I should. What do you think?"

Elizabeth winced. "Actually, I don't think you should go," she said. "To the symposium. Or to Berkeley, honestly."

"What?" Tia stopped walking and stared open-mouthed at Elizabeth.

"Seriously, Tee." Elizabeth halted and turned to face her. "I think you should give up your spot and give Evan a real chance. He really wants this, and I'm not sure you do. I don't think you're really being fair here."

Tia couldn't even speak. Where did Elizabeth get off, telling her what to do with her life? She hadn't been too shocked by Jade's reaction, but even sensible, reasonable Elizabeth thought she was being an evil person?

"Look, I don't remember asking your opinion about what college I should go to," Tia said.

Elizabeth just stared back at her, shocked.

"Forget it," Tia muttered. She spun around and stalked down the hall toward her next class. When did this become Pick-on-Tia Day?

Melissa hung her silk blouse on the gym-locker hook, then slipped on her gray sweatshirt. Another day. Another afternoon of cheerleading hell.

She used to really look forward to cheerleading practice. It was when she felt her most powerful—surrounded by her friends, doing all her best moves. She loved strutting her stuff at the games, but everyone was really there to watch the team. Practice, on the other hand, was where she got to preside. Tia might technically be captain, but Melissa had her entire gang to do her bidding—and she knew how to use them.

Had. Past tense. It was all different now.

As she pulled her hair back into a tight ponytail, she could hear Cherie behind her, screeching with laughter.

"God, we had the best time Friday night," Cherie squealed, extra loudly. "I can't believe we closed down First and Ten. And let's just say the night didn't end there for me and Aaron."

"Yeah, it's so obvious that he *really* likes you," Gina added.

Melissa concentrated on lacing up her sneakers, trying hard not to laugh. Did they really think she was going to be jealous over Aaron Dallas? Please!

"And wasn't Will's news so exciting?"

Here it goes, Melissa thought, bracing herself. Looked like they'd be using most of their practice energy trying to upset her. Why would today be any different? She was proud of how well she was keeping it together, refusing to give them the satisfaction of seeing her upset. But she wished her gut wouldn't twist up at the mention of Will. It was like some automatic reflex left over from the years she wasted on the guy. She was supposed to be over him. She was supposed to be moving on and focusing on her future—so how come her stomach didn't know it?

"Oh, I know." Cherie went on screeching toward

Melissa. "I think it's so great that Will's going to NYU. I mean, I hate that it's so far away, but he's so excited about it."

Melissa's hands started to tremble. Did she say Will was going to *NYU*? Since when? For years his only college plans had been to go wherever she went. Now all of a sudden he'd decided that *New York* was where he belonged? That was only supposed to be a backup. And why was he making up his mind so fast anyway?

"I bet he'll be *the* choice guy on campus," Gina added. "Just think of all the hot NYU girls he'll get to choose from. He'll be living it up so much, we'll probably never hear from him again."

Melissa felt the air squeeze out of her. She was glad she was stooped way over, tying up her tennis shoe. Otherwise they'd have definitely noticed the pain on her face.

So Will was moving on—all the way across the nation, in fact. Obviously all those years together hadn't mattered a bit to him. All those times they'd talked about walking hand in hand through campus, meeting up for lunch, sneaking into each other's dorms at night—well, they must not have meant anything to him. Looked like it would never happen now.

Melissa managed to finish the knot on one shoe and moved on to the other. This was stupid. She shouldn't care where Will went to college. Besides, she was definitely going to Smith, and no way could he follow her there. If only it were happening tomorrow. All this mindless high-school drama was messing with her mind.

She might have a future locked up at a great East Coast school, but that wasn't going to help her get through all the cheerleading practices left in the school year. . . .

Wait a sec. A smile slowly swept across her face. That was it! Hello, brilliant solution.

In a flash Melissa was pulling off her sneakers and sweats and getting back into her school clothes. Out of the corner of her eye she could see her former friends point at her and hear them snicker to one another.

As Melissa buttoned up her blouse, Tia suddenly appeared next to her. "Uh, Melissa? What are you doing?"

"Getting dressed," Melissa said matter-of-factly.

"Right," Tia said with a tight smile, as if Melissa were some five-year-old kid. "But, um . . . we're about to practice."

"Not me." Melissa was feeling lighter and stronger with every new piece of clothing. Why hadn't she thought of this sooner? She didn't need cheerleading anymore. There were no friends for her here, no fun, nothing to gain. Besides, now that she was a Smith girl, she should focus on more important things than hopping around in a short skirt during basketball games.

The door to the locker room banged open and Coach Laufeld entered, clipboard in hand. "All right, girls. Listen up," she barked out. "I want you guys here half an hour before the game tomorrow night. We'll have—" She paused and glared at Melissa. "Fox? Why aren't you dressed yet?"

All eyes turned toward her. To her right, she could see Cherie and the gang huddled together, watching her. To her left, Tia and the rest kept exchanging confused glances. Melissa paused briefly to savor the moment. Then she looked right at Coach Laufeld and said, "I'm not suiting up because I'm quitting the team."

A hum of gasps and whispers welled up around her. Melissa had to force herself not to smile.

"Quitting the team?" Coach Laufeld repeated in a monotone. She sighed. "Fox, we don't have time for this little drama right now. I want you to suit up and meet us on the gym floor in five minutes. Got that?"

Melissa tried to look as solemn as possible. "I'm sorry, Coach Laufeld, but I can't. I really am quitting. I'm going to be too busy getting ready for college."

The whispers grew louder. Coach Laufeld glanced around at the others. "Quiet!" she snapped. Then she turned back to Melissa. "Fox, do you realize that we have a halftime show to practice? A show that involves you? You are the top of the pyramid. You are the featured tumbler. And you are supposed to lead several cheers."

Again she tried hard not to grin. So they needed her, huh? Suddenly she was *amazingly* important to the squad. Well, this was what they got. They'd just have to do their best without her.

"Sorry, Coach Laufeld," she repeated, "but I'm not changing my mind."

Coach Laufeld's eyes bored into Melissa. "Well, then," she said, her clipboard whacking her whistle as she crossed her arms across her chest. "I guess there's no point in practice today, is there? The rest of you girls might as well get dressed and go home. I'll revise the halftime routine, and we'll run through it tomorrow before the game."

The other girls just stood there, looking at one another.

"That's all, gang. Move!" Coach Laufeld barked, and the rest of the squad began undressing. Coach then turned to Melissa, her face and voice becoming diplomatically polite. "Miss Fox, may I speak to you in my office for a second? I'd like to see if we could work something out."

Melissa shrugged halfheartedly. "Okay," she said,

and followed Coach Laufeld out the door. She was up for a good round of begging. It wasn't as if she had anything else to do. Besides, no matter what anyone said, she knew she wouldn't be changing her mind.

Evan let out a giant yawn as he walked toward House of Java. The day at school had seemed like it would never end, and now he just felt foggy. What he needed was a gigantic cup of his special coffee with an extra teaspoon of unrefined sugar.

As he approached the entrance, he could hear the door chimes tinkle, and the glass door suddenly swung open. A familiar figure in a black leather jacket stepped out, cradling a large, steaming to-go cup in between his hands.

"Hey, Conner," Evan greeted him.

Conner glanced up, his brown hair ruffling in the wind as he squinted at Evan. "Oh, hey," he said. "I was looking around for you at school."

"Yeah?" Evan asked. "What for?"

"There's going to be a concert just outside Twenty-Nine Palms on Wednesday night. I get to open for that LA band, the Pixels." Conner's green eyes flashed as he talked. "There's even going to be a reviewer for the *Times* out there and everything."

"Sounds cool," Evan said, grinning. Normally Conner was about as talkative as a caveman. It was strange to hear so many words from him at once.

"So, you want to come along?" Conner asked. "We're hitting the road right after school."

"I don't know." Evan shoved his hands into the front pocket of his woven parka and leaned against the brick wall. That heavy, familiar stress he'd been carrying around seemed to be pulling him inside out. "See, there's this Berkeley symposium thing I've been thinking about going to, and it's also Wednesday night."

"Right." Conner suddenly hunched his shoulders. His revved-up expression disappeared, replaced by his typically stoic gaze. "Well, I better go." He quickly stepped around Evan and stalked toward his vintage Mustang. "See ya," he called over his shoulder.

"Yeah. Good luck," Evan called, but Conner's retreat was too quick for him to hear.

Evan blew out his breath and let his head sag against the brick wall. That was strange. Conner seemed particularly ready to take off as soon as Berkeley was mentioned. That couldn't be a coincidence.

Conner was probably just avoiding anything emotional—as usual. Unless . . . a sinking sensation came over Evan . . . was Conner taking Tia's side?

It's just not fair, he thought, shaking his head. It was bad enough that his dream school turned him down flat. But now his close friends were suddenly acting all weird around him—as if he were some sort of vulture circling over Tia's bouncy little head.

At least some people were on his side. Jade was one hundred percent behind him, but she always got so worked up about it, he almost didn't like to open up to her. Elizabeth had seemed firmly behind him too—but every time he tried to talk to her about it, they got interrupted by Jessica or Jeff.

Evan pushed off from the wall and headed back to his car. Forget caffeine. He really didn't want to be in public right now. Besides, just thinking about his lousy life was enough of a jolt to his system.

To: ev-man@swiftnet.com
From: lizw@cal.rr.com
Subject: Sorry

Hi, Ev. Sorry I couldn't get back to you before now. Things have been crazy. I hope you're feeling better. By the way, remember that party this Friday that I told you and Jade about? Well, I thought you'd want to know it's mainly going to be Big Mesa people. So . . . Trent and Tia will probably be there. Not that you guys can't go or anything. I just thought you'd want to know.

Andy Marsden

<u>Notes for a New Routine</u>

So I have these two good friends. One is a radical, ultraliberal social-activist type, and the other is a cheerleader. Guess which one just got accepted by Berkeley? Wrong!

(Wait. That's not funny.)

Did you hear about Berkeley's new admission standards? Their new idea of the perfect student is a cheerleader who thinks the Dalai Lama is the South American relative of a camel.

(No! Not funny, plus it makes Tia sound like a ditz—which she's not.)

So I know this guy. He has two good friends. One just got into Berkeley but isn't sure she wants to go. The other is dying to get into Berkeley but got rejected. So this guy sort of sees both sides. He'd like to help them out, but he knows if he does, he'd probably end up losing both friends. . . .

Forget it. This is impossible. Maybe I should just focus on some good knock-knock jokes.

CHAPTER

Score One for the

6

Loiterer

"Can you believe Melissa?" Jessica asked as she and Tia left the locker room. "She actually quit the squad!"

"I know." Tia shook her head in disbelief. "That's got to be a bad, apocalyptic sign or something. Maybe there's an ancient scroll buried somewhere that says if Melissa Fox quits cheerleading, the world will end."

"Do you think all those rumors are true?" Jessica asked, glancing over her shoulder to see if anyone else was around. "Do you think she actually tried to cheat on Will with Aaron?"

Tia leaned sideways and unraveled her braid. "Hey, when it comes to Melissa Fox—*anything* is possible. Besides, it's so obvious that her gal pals are shutting her out."

"Yeah." Jessica pursed her lips thoughtfully. She had to admit it was somewhat satisfying to see Melissa endure the same sort of smear fest she'd put Jessica through last fall. But no matter how tough Melissa acted on the outside, Jessica knew it had to be getting to her. And Melissa tended to go a little crazy when things got tough. There was the suicide attempt last fall. And the last time she and Will had problems, Melissa had gotten mixed up with that dangerous SVU guy and Jessica, of all people, had to come to her rescue. She seriously hoped Melissa wasn't considering doing something stupid like that again.

"Hey, I've got a great idea!" Tia sang out, grabbing Jessica's wrist. "How about you and I drive over to Big Mesa and crash their basketball practice? We could cheer on Trent and Jeremy!"

Jessica felt a tug of longing. She smiled as she envisioned Jeremy's face lighting up as she and Tia walked into their gym. She really hadn't seen much of him lately. . . . But she couldn't do it. She had responsibilities.

"Sorry," she said. "I'm supposed to meet Liz at Le Chateau after practice. We're hoping to book a couple of tables for my parents' silver anniversary party."

"Can't you just go for a little while? I really want to talk to you about this whole Berkeley thing some more too," Tia pleaded, her big brown eyes wide. "Please? Just until the time practice would have been over?"

Again Jessica felt strongly tempted. Maybe she could race to Big Mesa, listen to Tia, stomp and cheer for Jeremy, steal a quick kiss from him, and then race to Le Chateau?

She sighed. "No. I better not," she replied, shaking her head. "Can we talk later? I really shouldn't risk being late. This is too big a deal."

"Sure. I understand," Tia said with a sigh. She turned and headed toward the parking lot. "I guess I'll see you tomorrow, then."

"Tell Jeremy I said hi," Jessica called after her. She watched as Tia disappeared through the double-glass doors. Then, glancing around the empty student center, she shouldered her gym bag and strolled down the corridor to the *Oracle* office.

The closed office door was practically throbbing from the activity inside the room. Jessica raised her hand to knock, then stopped herself. She checked her watch. There was still almost an hour left before Elizabeth was supposed to meet her. If she went inside, she would only be in the way. Besides, the thought of listening to all those journalist types blah, blah, blah about headline sizes didn't exactly appeal to her.

No, she might as well bum around somewhere until it was time to meet at the restaurant. In fact, there were lots of cool boutiques down by Le Chateau. She could do some shopping and still be on time to meet Elizabeth.

Jessica zipped up her jacket and walked toward the exit. Her pace quickened as she mentally listed the clothes and jewelry she needed to stock up on.

Hmmm. Maybe being responsible wasn't so bad after all.

Jeff's grip is so soft and firm as he holds her hand. She can sense his strength holding her up as they glide over the ice. Elizabeth's nose tingles from the cold, but the rest of her is warm. Gradually they accelerate. As their surroundings blur past them, she turns and focuses on Jeff's chiseled profile. She listens to the sound of his breathing and the light chip, chip *noises of their skates. They are alone in their own frozen paradise. Nothing else exists. . . .*

"Liz? Hey, Liz? How do you spell *valedictorian?*" Megan's freckled face loomed in front of her, snapping Elizabeth from her thoughts.

"Huh?" She sat up straight and blinked her surroundings into focus. "Oh. Um, it's *v-a-l-e-d-i-c-t-o-r-i-a-n.*"

"Thanks," Megan said with a grin. "So you must be working on something pretty tough. You looked like you were really thinking hard."

"Yeah, these cutlines can drive you crazy," Elizabeth replied. "Sometimes it's hard to find the perfect words."

Megan gave a brisk nod of understanding and walked back to her seat.

Elizabeth sighed and pushed the hair away from her face. Okay, so she lied. No need to tell Megan she'd been mentally twirling on an ice rink with her boyfriend for the past fifteen minutes. She squinted down at the stack of photos in her hand, trying to restart the logical part of her brain. It was time to get with it.

For some reason, school had been really boring today. It had been near impossible to pay attention in her classes, and her *Oracle* tasks were just one huge annoyance. Elizabeth felt like she'd swallowed a strong sedative. All she wanted to do was lie her head down and think about Jeff. Maybe this was what everyone referred to as "senioritis."

"Hey, Liz!"

Elizabeth glanced up and saw Maria rushing toward her.

"What's up?" Elizabeth asked once Maria reached her desk.

Maria plopped down in the chair beside her and took a deep breath. "I was just in the office getting a quote from the principal when someone called the school, looking for you."

"For me?" Elizabeth frowned. Who could that have been? No one would bother calling her here—unless it was a real emergency.

Maria read her anxiety. "Don't worry, it wasn't anything bad," she went on. "The receptionist said it was someone from the *Scope*. Apparently they're having some sort of crisis and wanted to know if you could go over there and help out."

"The *Scope*?" Elizabeth felt a rush of excitement. The magazine was really starting to rely on her. Obviously they must think she was professional and responsible enough to count on in a desperate situation.

"You should go right now," Maria said.

"You think so?" Elizabeth asked, wrinkling her brow. "But what about all these cutlines?"

"*I'll* do them," Maria said. She reached over and grabbed the photos out of Elizabeth's hands. "Go on," she added, grinning and nodding toward the door. "Go do some *real* work with a *real* publication."

"Thanks." Elizabeth smiled gratefully. Of course Maria would understand. "I promise to do something incredibly nice and selfless for you sometime soon."

"Just mention me when you win your Pulitzer," Maria said, laughing. "Now, get out."

Elizabeth grabbed her backpack and ran out the door. The sluggish feeling she'd had earlier was completely gone. Now she was wired for action, her mind conjuring up incredible scenarios of what might happen at the *Scope*. She imagined them thrusting a portable tape player in her hands and sending her out to do a key cover story. Or explaining to her why she was the perfect person to interview a major celebrity. Whatever it was, she'd show them her stuff.

She was just entering the parking lot when a thought came slamming into her: *Jessica*. They were supposed to meet at the restaurant in about half an hour.

Spinning around, she reentered the building and headed toward the gymnasium. Jessica would just have to understand that she couldn't make it today. The magazine was counting on her.

Elizabeth threw open one of the gym doors and looked inside. To her surprise, the place was empty. The lights were on, but no cheerleaders. No Jessica.

Maybe they were all getting dressed. Elizabeth headed over to the locker-room door but found it locked.

"What the . . . ?" she said, pulling the handle a few more times. Weird. Elizabeth walked out of the gym and glanced up and down the hallway, looking for a friendly face.

Cherie Reese was standing at her open locker. She was staring into a small compact mirror while applying bright red lipstick.

Elizabeth sighed. *Okay. I'll settle for an* un*friendly face.*

"Hey, Cherie? What happened to cheerleading practice?" she asked, pointing toward the gym.

"It got canceled," Cherie replied, her lips barely moving.

"Canceled?" Elizabeth repeated. "So where's Jessica?"

Cherie snapped her compact shut and glared at

Elizabeth. "How should I know?" she retorted.

Ookay. Elizabeth spun around and headed back toward the exit. Lots of help she was.

In the parking lot she noticed the Jeep was already gone. So Jessica was definitely not on campus. *Oh, well,* Elizabeth thought as she hopped into her mother's silver Avalon. When she got to *Scope,* she'd just call Le Chateau and try to reach Jessica there.

If Jessica remembered to show up.

"Wow," Jessica breathed. She held up the plum-colored blouse by her chin and lifted the sleeves with her arms. Then she studied her reflection in a nearby mirror. Yes! This was *exactly* what she'd been searching for. It was just the right color and would go perfectly with those pants she got at the mall last week.

She turned the price tag over in her hand. *Oops . . .* then again . . .

"May I help you?"

Jessica looked up as a young, female salesclerk strode up to her. In her swanky slip dress, teardrop earrings, and upswept hairdo, she looked like she was dressed for an opera instead of work.

"Thanks, but I'm just looking," Jessica replied, carefully returning the blouse to its rack.

"I see." The woman continued to smile at Jessica without actually smiling. "I'm afraid we don't allow people to loiter inside here. If you are serious about making a purchase, I'd be happy to help you find something. Otherwise I'll have to ask you to leave." She did a brisk about-face and trotted back to the front of the store.

Well, excuse moi, Jessica thought, grimacing at the woman's retreating back. She realized her Sweet Valley High letter jacket probably didn't scream "large sales commission," but still! Miss No Loitering didn't have to act like Jessica was covered in bugs.

Jessica zipped up her jacket and slowly sauntered past the saleswoman and out the door. So much for some quality shopping. That made two chichi clothing boutiques, a jewelry store, and a fancy shoe shop she'd been oh-so-politely booted out of this afternoon. People were definitely friendlier at the mall. Jessica wondered what would happen if freak hurricane-strength winds forced her to take shelter in one of these places. Would they help her out or smile and say, "Sorry, no loiterers," before pushing her back out into the elements?

"Forget them," she mumbled to herself as she started down the sidewalk. When she became a rich and famous actress, she would never shop there. That would show those snobs. Besides, their stuff wasn't that great anyway.

She checked her watch. It was almost time to meet Elizabeth. She supposed she could just wait around in the restaurant lobby until her sister showed up. She couldn't wait to tell Elizabeth about all the rude sales-clerks. Her sister would be appropriately outraged. Maybe after checking out Le Chateau they could go purposely bug those people. Or maybe Elizabeth could pretend she was doing a story for the *Scope*! Jessica chuckled as she pictured several well-dressed salesladies tripping over each other while trying to please them.

Whatever they ended up doing, she and Elizabeth should definitely hang out. It had been way too long since they'd done anything together. She missed hav-ing fun with her twin.

Jessica walked down the block to the restaurant, a converted Victorian manor. She pushed through the door into an ornate, polished hardwood foyer. A man in a white suit stood behind a podium.

"May I help you?" he asked in a voice that seemed more suited for, "What do you want?" His brow fur-rowed as he looked her up and down.

Jessica smiled sweetly. She was not going to get kicked out of this place too. "I'm waiting for someone," she explained, sitting down on a gold-fringe-trimmed chaise lounge.

"Do you have a reservation?" he asked.

"No, but—"

"Then I'm afraid you'll have to go somewhere else. This is not a waiting area."

She glanced around at the chairs flanking the walls. "Then what are all these seats for?"

"They are for our customers," the man replied, overemphasizing the last word. "Again, do you have a reservation?"

"No, but we're—"

"Then I must ask you to leave. Several diners will be arriving soon for the dinner hour and we need to keep these spaces open."

Jessica stood and headed out the door. These people really had a knack for making her feel like a mangy stray dog. Why couldn't her parents' favorite restaurant be International House of Pancakes?

She walked down the porch steps and down the sidewalk. Spying a bench at a nearby bus stop, she quickly headed over and sat down. She still had a clear view of the restaurant, so she'd be able to see Elizabeth when she pulled up.

Jessica slouched back against the wrought-iron seat and blew on her hands. As the sun slowly dropped behind the line of trees, so did the temperature. She checked her watch. Elizabeth was five minutes late. That probably meant she'd show any second.

Twenty minutes and ten degrees later, Elizabeth still hadn't arrived. Jessica's toes were growing numb inside her boots, and she'd already irritated several bus drivers who had pulled over only to have her wave them on.

"Where *is* she?" Jessica asked as she sat forward and rubbed her palms together. She was definitely at the right place, she had definitely arrived in plenty of time, and there was no way Elizabeth could have entered the restaurant without her seeing. Something weird must have happened.

Maybe I should just leave, Jessica wondered. She was tired of cold weather and cold people. More than anything she wanted to go home, call Jeremy, and then take a long, warm bath. But what about the anniversary party? It was only three days away, and they hadn't done a thing to plan it. If they didn't get something in the works soon, it would never get pulled off. And her parents really deserved it too.

And they would get it.

Full of resolve, Jessica stood and marched toward the restaurant. As she pushed open the door, she was surprised to find the house magically transformed. The air was warm and full of the fragrance of flowers and fine food. All the chandeliers were on, lighting up the rooms with a soft, romantic glow. It was the perfect place for a special anniversary party.

"A-hem." She glanced up and saw the same white-suit guy frowning at her. Next to him sneered another man in a black coat and tie. Jessica took a deep breath and approached them.

"May I help you?" asked Dark Suit, barely containing his impatience.

"Yes. You can," Jessica replied, smiling warmly. "My sister and I are looking for a place to schedule a special silver-anniversary party for my parents. My parents have impeccable taste, and this is their favorite restaurant."

Dark Suit hardly looked convinced. He nodded over most of her words and gestured toward the exit. "Yes, well—" he began.

"Oh, and along with my family, we will have to accommodate several of my parents' very distinguished friends, many of whom eat here regularly," she continued, flashing an exact duplicate of the clothing-boutique saleswoman's blank smile. "I'm not sure how many. Let's see." She gazed up at the bead-board ceiling and began counting on her fingers. "There's Dr. Lyle Covington and his wife, Professor Galloway, Mrs. Barber, who runs the Barber Foundation—she's so nice, isn't she?—Mr. Fowler, the Applegates, oh, and who is that nice man who works for the mayor?" She tapped her fingers against her forehead, pretending to rack her brain.

Slowly Mr. Dark Suit's arm swerved from the direction of the exit toward the direction of the dining room. "Yes, well . . . I'm so sorry you had to wait," he said, quickly flashing White Suit an angry stare. "I'm certain we can accommodate your party. I'm Gerard, the maître d' of Le Chateau. Please allow me to show you around our establishment." He ducked his head in a humble sort of semibow and offered her his arm.

Jessica's grin widened. "Why, thank you, Gerard. That would be *so* kind."

Yes! she thought as she placed her hand on the crook of his arm and followed him into the main dining area. Score one for the loiterer!

Elizabeth Wakefield

Hello? Is this the host's station at Le Chateau? Yes, this is Elizabeth Wakefield calling again. Yes, I know I've already called twice before. Are you sure there's no one waiting in your reception area? No, I don't have a reservation. Yes, I know you don't allow loiterers, but could you please check again? No one? Has anyone called for me? The name is Elizabeth Wakefield. No? Well, then, could I leave a message? I know we don't have a reservation, but . . . Look, could I just speak with the maître d', please? You say he's busy? (Sigh.) Never mind. I guess she just forgot.

CHAPTER 7

Gurl Power

"It was so great, Jeff. The *Scope*'s articles editor was out with the flu!" Elizabeth raised her right shoulder to hold the phone to her ear as she reached down to pull off her shoes. "I mean, I feel bad for her and all, but it really gave me the chance to show them what I can do in a crisis."

"That's so cool," Jeff said. "So did they assign you another story?"

"Well, not exactly." Elizabeth flopped back on her bed. "They actually gave her article to one of their regular contributors, but they needed me to do the research for him since he was so busy with his other piece. And I did some fact checking and called people to arrange photo shoots. It was amazing. I felt like a real pro."

"You are a pro."

Elizabeth smiled and shut her eyes. She could imagine the look on his face—that sparkly glint his eyes got whenever he paid her a compliment. If only he were here right now.

"Thanks, but I'm not a pro yet," she said. "I still have loads to learn."

"You'll get there. I know it," he murmured. "All the magazines will be fighting over you. Everyone knows how smart and hardworking and responsible you are."

All of a sudden there was a sharp rap on the bedroom door. Immediately after, it swung open and Jessica came striding into the room, her cheeks flushed from anger.

"Excuse me just a sec, Jeff," Elizabeth said into the mouthpiece. *This is getting old,* she thought, pressing the phone against her and sitting up straight.

"Where were you?" they asked at the same time.

Jessica's eyes blinked wider. "Where was *I? I* was at the restaurant. Where were *you?*"

"I had to go in to the *Scope,*" Elizabeth explained. "One of their staff members was out sick, and they needed me to—"

"Spare me," Jessica said wearily, holding a hand out in front of her. "I'm cold and tired and hungry, and I'm really not in the mood for some more excuses. You know, you could have let me know if something came up."

"I tried!" Elizabeth threw up her left arm in frustration. "You left school before I could catch you. I tried calling the restaurant from the *Scope,* and they

107

said you weren't there. I just figured you'd forgotten all about it."

Jessica's mouth fell open, and her eyes narrowed into angry slits. "You figured I *forgot?*" she hissed.

"Well, it has been known to happen," Elizabeth said with a shrug.

For a moment Jessica just stood there, twitching slightly as her muscles tensed and untensed. Elizabeth wasn't sure if she would cry, scream, or begin throwing objects in her direction. Eventually Jessica shook her head at the floor and blew out her breath. "Forget it. I'm done," she said, her voice strangely hollow. She looked up and glared at Elizabeth. "Tell Steven that Airhead *somehow* managed to book a room at the restaurant for seven o'clock Thursday. I'm sure my *college-boy* brother and *superresponsible* sister can manage to invite the guests and get Mom and Dad over there. Since you guys can't count on me, you're free to take it from here!" With that, she turned and stomped out of the room, slamming the door behind her.

Elizabeth sat motionless as the sound waves rippled over her. Why did Jessica have to go all drama queen on her again? It wasn't her fault that the *Scope* needed her or that the restaurant people were useless when she called. Frankly, she did everything she could. Jessica was just freaking for no reason.

She'd be so glad when this anniversary thing was

over with. Her parents deserved it and all, but she really hated having to deal with her sister's hysterics. From now on she should spend more time with people who truly appreciated her—namely, her boyfriend.

Elizabeth put the receiver against her ear and settled back onto her bed. "Sorry about that, Jeff," she said with a grin. "So . . . where were we?"

The walls of the school gymnasium were quaking with noise as Will walked through the double doors. The stands were already packed, and the crowd was getting fired up with a loud spirit-building chant.

Stomp, stomp, clap! Stomp, stomp, clap! "Sweet Valley High will rock you!" they shouted.

Will paused. Maybe he shouldn't have come. Ever since his leg injury forced him to give up football, big events like this at Sweet Valley always sent him on a big self-pity trip. For some reason, though, he'd really wanted to be here tonight. After all, he should show support for the team. And there weren't many chances left to hang with his friends before the year was up. So maybe it was some sense of duty that brought him here.

Stomp, stomp, clap! Stomp, stomp, clap!

"Yay, Gladiators!" came a chorus of female shouts from the floor.

Will immediately tensed. One thing was for sure, he

109

definitely hadn't come to see Melissa. Watching her jump up and down with a huge grin on her face would only make him sick to his stomach. She'd probably be trying to catch his eye too, just to prove how happy and carefree she was without him in her life. He'd show her. He would spend the entire game looking elsewhere. He'd just pretend the cheerleaders didn't exist.

"Will! Over here!"

He glanced up to see Josh and Matt sitting on the team bench. Matt was waving toward an empty seat behind him on the first-row bleacher. It was usually reserved for team people, but the coaches had told him he was welcome to sit there anytime. Will walked over and sat down.

"What's up?" he said, leaning forward so the guys could hear him over the noise. "What'd I miss?"

"Nothing," Josh muttered as he scowled toward the gym floor. "They've really got their defense going, and we're only up by four."

"Come on! Stop him!" Matt shouted. He shook his arm at the opposing team's player who was breaking for the basket.

Will squinted out toward the playing floor, trying to lose himself in the game. Unfortunately, he couldn't push the cheerleaders' voices out of his mind as they chanted, "*R-e-b-o-u-n-d!*"

Okay. Maybe he would look at her—just once.

After all, if he purposely avoided her, she'd notice. Then she might think he still cared—which he didn't. What he needed to do was to act indifferent and let his eyes casually pass over her. That would prove that he was way beyond her now.

"Man!" Matt groaned as the opponent made an easy basket. The rest of the crowd grumbled collectively.

Will shook his head as if irritated while gradually letting his gaze wander toward the cheerleaders. Melissa was nowhere in sight. He peered more closely, checking their bench to see if she was taking a break, but she wasn't anywhere along the sidelines.

"Where is she?" he muttered.

"What?" Josh asked, following Will's gaze.

"Uh . . . " Will hadn't meant to say anything out loud. He quickly racked his brain for an explanation.

"You mean Melissa?" Matt asked, leaning backward. "Yeah, I was going to ask you that too. Why do you think she's not here?"

Will shrugged. "I don't know. I don't really care."

"Hey, there's Lila," Josh said. He pointed toward Lila, who stood over by the cheerleaders' bench, getting a drink. "Let's ask her."

Will was just about to say no when Matt whistled loudly and waved his arms. "Lila!" he called.

Lila looked up and frowned at him.

"Come here," Matt said, motioning with his hands.

Lila glanced around her, then quickly trotted toward their seats. "What do you want?" she asked, stooping down next to Will.

"Where's Melissa?" Matt asked, motioning toward the rest of the squad.

She looked right at Will. "Didn't you hear what happened?"

Will shook his head. "Are you kidding?" he said, trying to sound nonchalant. "I don't care what she does."

Again Lila checked around her. Then she leaned in close and raised an eyebrow. "Melissa quit the squad yesterday," she whispered.

"What?" Matt and Josh said in unison.

Will gaped at her, forgetting to act casual.

"Yeah, she really messed things up for us too," Lila went on. "Coach made us come two hours before the game so we could completely redo our routine."

"Why'd she quit?" Matt asked.

Lila rolled her eyes. "Oh, you know. She told Coach it's because she's going to Smith and this is all part of her newfound 'gurl power.' But everyone knows it's because no one would talk to her during practice."

"Man, what a wacko." Josh shook his head.

"Tell me about it," she said with a smirk. The crowd roared again, and Lila craned her neck around Matt's head to glance out at the gym floor. "I gotta get back down there. See ya, guys."

"Aw, man! They scored *again?*" Matt griped. "Coach needs to put us in and fast." He and Josh immediately tuned back in to the game.

Will watched Lila race back to the cheerleaders as they lined up for another rally cry. *Weird,* he thought, pursing his lips. First Melissa announced she was off to some all-girl school and now she quit the squad? This wasn't like her at all. Melissa didn't deal well with change, and suddenly she was purposely undoing everything in her life? This was a bad, bad sign. After riding with her through all the ups and downs of her past, Will knew it was only a matter of time before things really got to Melissa. And when that happened, there was no telling what she might do.

Maybe he should give her a call, just to make sure she was okay. It wasn't like he wanted her back or anything. He just felt a little bit responsible for her after so many years as her boyfriend. More than anyone, he would see her danger signs.

Then again, she could be just fine. Maybe she really did want to reinvent everything about herself. Or . . . maybe this was all a trap to get him worked up about her. Will shifted uncomfortably in his seat as the crowd stomped and cheered all around him.

No. He should definitely call her. That way he could ease his conscience and make sure she wouldn't pull anything stupid. *Then* he could go back to hating her.

Will reached out and tapped Matt. "Hey, guys, I gotta run. I just remembered something. Uh . . . my dad and I have to go over some forms for NYU."

Josh and Matt exchanged glances. "What did I tell you?" Josh asked, shaking his head. "He's turning into a total New Yorker already."

"Bet he starts rooting for the Knicks too," Matt put in, smiling slyly.

"Uh-uh," Will said as he got to his feet. "You guys know I'm a die-hard Laker fan. Some things you never get out of your system."

No. No. No. No. Yes. No. Maybe.

Melissa reached into her closet and pulled out a long-sleeved, apricot-colored wraparound shirt. Would this be the sort of thing a Smith girl would wear? She held it up against her chest and stared at her reflection in her antique cheval mirror. Hmmm. Probably not. Seemed a little too low cut.

She tossed the shirt onto a pile of clothing on her bed and continued sifting through the contents of her closet. It was amazing how much free time she had now with no friends, no boyfriend, and no cheerleading. Just this evening she'd had time to finish her homework, watch an hour of television, and polish her silver jewelry.

All that done, she was now thumbing through her wardrobe, trying to separate her "California" clothes from things she could wear at Smith.

She'd gotten the idea after perusing one of the glossy-colored college leaflets they'd sent her. It was plastered with photos of girls in woolen skirts, thick tights, and sweater sets. (Especially turtlenecks. For some reason, they really seemed to love turtlenecks.) It made her realize that she should probably adopt a more "preppy" look if she wanted to fit in on campus.

Flipping through her outfits, she was amazed at how few items she owned that were suitable. Thanks to a major difference in weather and attitude, her personal sense of style would have to be completely transformed. No more breezy dresses, floral prints, or spaghetti straps. No more funky thongs with capri pants. Hello, flannel, wool blazers, overcoats with knit scarves, and lots and lots of plaid.

Melissa reached into her closet and pulled out yet another flirty sundress, this one a pale pink Ann Taylor. She smiled faintly as she fingered the soft, sheer material. The last time she wore it was when she and Will celebrated their fifth anniversary as a couple. She remembered the way he looked at her across the candlelit table.

She turned around and quickly threw it onto the "no" pile. That had been forever ago—before she'd become a bona fide Smith girl. And before Will had decided his destiny lay in New York.

The phone on her desk started ringing. Melissa ignored it. There was absolutely no one she wanted to talk to right now.

She calmly considered her purple fluffy sweater coat as the answering machine picked up.

"Liss. It's me."

Will? Melissa's mouth fell open.

"Hey, listen. Lila told me that you quit cheerleading, and I just wanted to . . . well . . . I wanted to see if you were okay."

"What do you care?" she mumbled to herself. Great. Just when she had things all sorted out, he had to call and get her upset. She should go turn off the machine, or at least turn it down. Or pick up the phone and immediately hang up. She definitely didn't need to hear this right now.

For some reason, though, she couldn't move. She could only stand there and listen as if tied down to the spot.

"You know," he began, then paused, taking a deep breath, "I really think that was a mistake. It's like you're walking away from things and saying they don't matter when you know they do."

Melissa's blood began a slow simmer. What made him think he could tell her how to live her

116

life? She was doing great—no thanks to him.

"I mean, you might think you're punishing other people, but you're really punishing yourself," he continued. "Just because you've been accepted to some fancy East Coast school doesn't mean you should turn your back on stuff that's important to you here."

Melissa's eyes narrowed, and her hands clenched into fists. Suddenly the invisible force that held her there seemed to let go. Throwing the sweater onto the floor, she marched over to her phone and picked it up.

"And what about you, huh?" she snapped into the receiver. "Mr. *NYU*. Seems to me you've been turning your back on some people and *some plans* you made."

"Hey, Liss," he said calmly.

This made her even angrier. Had he known she was here listening? All of a sudden she felt like she'd stepped into a trap. "Don't 'hey' me," she said as evenly as possible. "You broke up with me, remember? That means you don't get to 'hey' me. You don't get to call me. And you don't get to boss me around."

"That's not it." Will's voice grew more urgent. "I just think you've been making too many big decisions too fast. I don't want you to, you know, lose it later on."

Melissa pressed her palm against her forehead. So *that* was it. He didn't really care what happened to her. He just didn't want to carry around any guilt if she pulled something crazy, like last time. "Save it," she hissed. "I'm not some psycho. Why don't you just hang with your friends and pack for New York and leave me alone!"

Before he could say anything further, she turned off the phone and tossed it onto the "no" pile of clothing.

Perfect, she thought. *Wish I could just as easily toss him out of my life—and mind.*

She paced around the room, unable to stand still. She wasn't sure if she was upset that he'd called and bugged her or that he'd done so only out of some sense of obligation. And since when did quitting cheerleading mean you were a nutcase? Were people always going to think of her as unstable just because of what happened last fall? It was so unfair. She'd been doing an amazing job of holding it all together—at least until *he* called.

Thank God she was getting away from this place and everyone in it. She bet everyone at Smith wouldn't judge her.

Melissa walked over to her desk and stared down at the large manila envelope from Smith. She was so glad she'd applied there. Had she somehow known, deep down, that it would be the one? Had fate stepped in? As she picked up the envelope for a closer look, a small card bearing the Smith College logo fell onto the floor. She snatched it up and studied it.

You are cordially invited . . . , it read in fancy script. It went on to give information about a local women's studies seminar sponsored by Smith College that would take place the next evening at a nearby lecture hall.

Hmmm, Melissa thought. *Fate again?* She should definitely go. Hanging out with some other strong, independent-thinking women was just what she needed right now.

Besides, it wasn't like she had anything else to do.

Will slammed the receiver down on its base and kicked his bed with his good leg. He actually left a basketball game for *this?*

Once again, he couldn't believe Melissa. Here he'd called to check up on her, admitting he was concerned, and she made it seem like he was doing something awful. Fine. From now on he was going to completely stop caring. Melissa could go to Smith, or join a cult, or disappear over the Bermuda Triangle and it wouldn't bother him in the least.

Plus he had his own future to plan for. So what if Melissa was reinventing herself as a "gurl-power" Smith type? He was going off to NYU as a new person too. He'd be in a brand-new place with brand-new goals, completely free from his ex-girlfriend and all of her games.

So what was he waiting for anyway? Will spun

around and stalked over to his desk, rummaging through the top drawer until he found what he was looking for: the NYU acceptance letter. He pushed back his chair, sat down, snatched a pen out of his Los Angeles Raiders coffee mug, and quickly filled in the blanks.

There! he thought triumphantly after he'd written the final piece of information. *That was easy.*

He slowly stood up and perused the form, his anger completely evaporated. So there it was. His future. His freedom. His ticket out of Sweet Valley. Right there in his hands. There was no stopping him now.

Except . . . Will scratched his head and slowly sank back down into the chair. He really should double-check his answers and make sure it was all correct.

He leaned forward and carefully read and reread the letter. Nope. There were absolutely no mistakes whatsoever. He'd done a good job. Everything was a go.

Okay, then. He sat way back in his chair and drummed his fingers on the arm. Guess it was time to mail it.

Then again, he still needed a stamp.

Will searched through every drawer in his desk but came up empty. What could he do now? He couldn't mail it without a stamp. Oh, well. Guess he'd have to wait after all.

Although he could ask his parents for a stamp. If they were still awake. Of course, that meant he should probably tell them he'd decided on New York University. They'd been so excited for him that he got in, but they had some mixed feelings since it would mean him going so far away. Still, he was sure they'd be happy to know his choice.

He headed down the hall to his father's study. The light shining out from underneath the door told him his dad was still awake and available. Will knocked softly.

"Come in," his dad called.

Will poked his head inside. "Hey, Dad? Are you really busy? 'Cause if you are, I can come back later."

His father laughed. "No, of course I'm not too busy." He set his book down next to him. "What do you need?"

"I, um." Will slowly glanced around the room. "I need to borrow a stamp."

Mr. Simmons's brow furrowed. "What for?"

"To mail an acceptance letter," Will replied, fiddling with the knob on the door. "I've, uh . . . I've decided to go to NYU."

His dad's eyes grew wide, and he slowly sat forward in his chair. "New York? Really?" he asked. "Are you sure about this? Don't you think we should discuss it a little more?"

Will paused and took a deep breath. "NYU is my top choice."

"Since when?" Mr. Simmons asked, frowning.

Will shrugged. "For a while now. It's got a great journalism school. And it's right in the middle of everything. It's probably the coolest place in the world for someone who wants to be a sports journalist."

For a moment Mr. Simmons just stared at Will intently, as if searching for something in his expression. Will forced himself not to look away. His throat felt dry, and his legs were all shaky. What was wrong with him? He really did feel that way about NYU. So why was his dad making him feel all guilty?

Finally his dad let out a long sigh and stood up. "Well, if you're one hundred percent sure that this is what you want, then your mother and I will support you." He reached out his hand and smiled. "I'm proud of you, son. It's an excellent school, and they'd be lucky to have you."

Will swallowed hard. "Thanks," he whispered as he shook his dad's outstretched palm. He was glad his dad stopped the Q and A, but for some reason, the tightness in his stomach was still there.

"So now all you need is a stamp, huh? Well, I think I can help you out there." He leaned over and began rummaging through the drawers of his executive desk. "Hmmm. I thought I had some right here." He tried another drawer, then checked his wallet.

Finally he turned toward Will and shook his head. "Sorry, son. I guess I'm flat out."

"Oh, that's okay," Will replied, feeling a surge of relief. "I don't have to mail it tonight. Good night, Dad."

"Good night, Will."

Will shut the door to the study and went back to his room. Guess it wasn't meant to happen tonight after all. He'd just have to stop at the post office tomorrow after school.

If he had time.

Lila Fowler

So Will's asking about Melissa, huh? Interesting . . . Of course, he made it sound so innocent and all, but I could tell what was really up. I'm sure Josh and Matt were too dense to notice the worry in his eyes. Something tells me Will isn't as over Melissa as he wants us to think.

Of course Cherie is acting all queen bee these days—as if she gets to inherit all of Melissa's power just because she happened to witness her downfall. She ought to watch her back. So far it <u>seems</u> like Melissa's reign is over for good, but Cherie shouldn't write her off too quickly. Melissa's like one of those bad blockbuster movies. Just when you think you've seen the last of one, another, even worse version pops up.

I'm as glad as anyone that Melissa got knocked flat. But you know, Cherie isn't any better at playing top girl. Just to play things safe, I think I'll be keeping some distance from her. Any day now <u>Melissa II</u> might hit theaters, especially if Will has a hand in her resurrection.

CHAPTER
no Brainless Bimbo
8

Melissa strode into the large, wood-paneled lecture hall. A thick cardboard sign on a chair read, Smith College Women's Studies Group. Pausing just inside the doorway, she carefully studied the assembled crowd. Approximately twenty girls sat in chairs arranged in a circle at the front of the room. It surprised her that not everyone was a superprep. A couple of girls were wearing long embroidered dresses that looked like they were made in India or Guatemala. One girl even wore a black leather ensemble and sported a nose ring.

The room felt hot and stuffy. Taking off her thick, burgundy cardigan, Melissa picked lint off her own black turtleneck and corduroy skirt. Then she slipped her hand inside the neck of her shirt and scratched her collarbone. Wool always made her itch. She was glad she'd done such excellent research on the dressing habits of a typical Smith girl—she definitely looked like she belonged—but she was somehow going to have to grow thicker skin before classes started that fall.

She scanned the area and spotted a couple of empty chairs near the center aisle. Melissa sat in one and gazed around for someone to gossip with. After all, she figured she should find some new friends while she was there. Some smart, independent girls she could hang out with until she escaped small-minded Sweet Valley for college. She tuned in to the conversation on her left.

"Empiricism? No way!" shrieked a short-haired girl in a red turtleneck. "How would you experience an atom?"

"*Inner* experience," replied the leather-clad girl, smacking her chewing gum. "I'm talking inner experience."

Ookay, Melissa thought, facing forward again. Maybe she could find some more exciting people to talk to. She leaned to her right and tried to overhear the chatter in that direction. Because of the empty chair on that side of her, she couldn't quite hear everything. But after making out a few words like *European market, globalization,* and *the GATT treaty,* she quickly realized it wasn't her scene either.

She straightened back up and scowled. *Is everyone here boring?* she wondered, reaching up to scratch the back of her neck. *Or did I just choose the seat next to all the losers?*

It wasn't that she didn't feel smart enough for the crowd. She knew what the GATT treaty was, and she vaguely remembered studying the empiricists in her world-lit class. It was just that outside of school, she really didn't want to discuss those things. Melissa scanned the faces of the girls around her. Someone there must want to talk about something normal.

At that moment a girl in a long Laura Ashley–type dress breezed into the empty seat and bent over to set a large brown case on the floor. Melissa squinted at her. She seemed normal enough. Long, ash blond hair, round John Lennon glasses, and an almost-but-not-quite-pretty freckled face.

"Hi," Melissa greeted her, smiling warmly. "I'm Melissa."

"I'm Theresa," the girl replied, lifting her chin to let her hair fall back off her shoulders.

"So," Melissa began, searching for a neutral topic. She really hoped the girl didn't want to discuss molecular biology or anything. "You're thinking about Smith?"

"Of course," she replied, her face expressionless. "It's where my mother went."

"Really? That's cool," Melissa replied. "So you must have the inside scoop, huh? What's Smith like? Is it fun?"

Theresa shrugged. "I guess so."

"I wonder if it's really strict there. I just hope they don't have a dress code or anything. Of course"— Melissa lowered her voice and nodded toward the body-piercing girl—"she probably does too, huh?"

Theresa glanced over at Leather Girl, looked back at Melissa, and shrugged again.

What's with this girl? Melissa wondered. She was beginning to wish she'd joined the globalization talk. She blew out her breath and stared down at the floor, her eyes resting on the large, odd-shaped box next to the girl's chair. "What's that?" she asked, pointing.

For the first time since she'd arrived, Theresa smiled. "It's a French horn case," she replied, her eyes lighting up. "I just left practice. Do you play in band?"

Melissa shook her head. "No. I'm a cheerleader."

Theresa's face dimmed. "Oh," she said in an empty voice.

"I mean, I *was* a cheerleader," Melissa went on, shaking her head and laughing. "I had to quit the squad to focus on preparing for college and all."

Theresa nodded slightly but barely made eye contact. Then she sighed and glanced around the circle at the rest of the girls.

I can't believe it, Melissa thought. *She actually seems bored talking to* me.

At that moment a redheaded woman wearing glasses and a perfectly tailored navy blue suit walked through a door next to the blackboard. "Good evening," she greeted. She nodded approvingly at the crowd in front of her. "It's good to see so many women here tonight."

Women? Melissa thought. That was a switch. She almost didn't feel old enough to be referred to as a "woman," yet she liked the term. It made her feel more powerful somehow. And lately she needed to feel that as much as possible.

"My name is Professor Ashworth, and I'm head of the Women's Studies Department at Smith," the woman continued as she sat down in one of the chairs along with the audience. "I have written two books on the role of the modern woman," the professor went on. "I'm a fiend for anything dark chocolate. And my all-time personal heroine is Jane Goodall, who is not only a champion of the environment and animal rights, but also overcame sexist and educational stereotyping to rise to the top of her scientific community."

Several people in the crowd nodded appreciatively. A few of them even clapped. Melissa smiled brightly.

"Now I'd like to hear about all of you." The professor crossed her legs, rested her elbow on her knee, and leaned forward, chin in hand. "Let's go around the circle, one by one. Please give us your name, tell us a little about yourself, and name your own personal heroine."

The girl on the professor's right stood up and cleared her throat. She was the one wearing an exotic-looking woven dress. "Hello. My name is Minerva Gaskill. I am a vegetarian, except that I do eat fish. I love doing yoga. And my heroine has always been Mother Teresa."

Professor Ashworth beamed at the girl. A few murmurs of approval welled up from the crowd. Melissa groaned inwardly. Mother Teresa? Okay, she was definitely a great person and all, but come on! Could she *be* more obvious?

The professor stared expectantly at the next person— a petite, mousy-looking girl in a gray wool skirt and a white blouse buttoned all the way up to the collar. "Hi. Um . . . I'm Ali Moser." Everyone leaned forward and strained to hear. "And, um, I like reading and playing chess and riding horses. My heroine is Eleanor Roosevelt."

Melissa rolled her eyes. Were these girls (or "women") for real? It suddenly seemed like she was in fifth grade again, and everyone was choosing historical figures guaranteed to please the teacher. She studied Dr. Ashworth as the next person stood to speak. The professor seemed casual and friendly, and she was definitely trying to make people feel at ease. But there was still something about her that made her stand out—something besides her smart suit and designer eyeglasses. Dr. Ashworth gave off a certain attitude Melissa understood. It was the vibe of someone who liked to succeed, but on her own terms.

That could be me in twelve years, she thought, watching the professor closely. She found herself wondering if the woman was married or had a boyfriend. Melissa guessed not. She envisioned Dr. Ashworth going on lots of dates with different kinds of exciting and powerful men—but no serious relationship. She was probably way too busy and fulfilled for that sort of thing.

Melissa grinned at the images in her mind, superimposing her own face over that of the professor. Professor Fox. Dr. Fox. That definitely had a ring to it.

A preppy type had just named Representative Pat Schroeder as her all-time heroine, and the rest of the crowd was muttering their consent. *Yeah, yeah,* Melissa thought while smiling and nodding. Another great woman, but another way too obvious choice. Wait until they heard who *her* heroine was. She'd end up standing out in the crowd after all. And she'd probably score all sorts of brownie points with Dr. Ashworth.

Just one more person and then it would be her turn.

"My name is Theresa Givens," said the girl beside her. "I love music and play four different kinds of instruments." She lifted her chin and pushed her wire-rimmed glasses farther up on her nose.

Goody for you, Melissa thought, shifting anxiously in her seat. *Just get on with it.*

"And I would have to say," the girl went on, "that the woman who inspired me the most in my life, besides my mother, is Helen Keller."

Melissa nervously wiggled her foot as she waited for the crowd to quiet again. Then she calmly rose to her feet and smiled at the group. "My name is Melissa Fox," she announced. "I love wildflowers, romantic comedies, and gymnastics. And my all-time biggest heroine is . . ." She paused and took a breath. "Natasha B.!"

Her satisfied smile wavered as she glanced around at the others' faces. Some were staring at her blankly, their mouths slightly open. Others looked back at her with their jaws set and their foreheads deeply furrowed. *Oh, don't tell me,* Melissa thought. *These straitlaced types have no idea who she is!*

Well, that could be fixed. She smiled primly. "Of course, you all know that Natasha B. is a successful entrepreneur, designer, philanthropist, and trendsetter," she added. "But she is probably best known as the creator of the can't-live-without lip gloss—Lip Glacé."

Again her remarks were met with complete silence. Her skin itched violently as she glanced from face to face, searching for a friendly expression to latch onto. But no one would meet her gaze. Each person was either carefully averting her eyes or exchanging a smirk with someone else. Melissa's throat tightened as an eerie feeling of déjà vu settled over her. She was suddenly reminded of being back in the Sweet Valley locker room, surrounded by snide laughter.

She turned to gauge Dr. Ashworth's reaction. Surely *she* appreciated Melissa's unique perspective.

Dr. Ashworth smiled at her, but it was a tight, well-mannered type of grin. The professor cleared her throat and recrossed her legs. "Well," she began.

Melissa sensed she was being dismissed. But she wasn't ready to sit back down yet. She had to explain herself. She couldn't let these people think she was a brainless bimbo. "Okay," she said, folding her arms and scratching both elbows simultaneously. "I know it's not exactly helping lepers or anything," she began with a shaky laugh. "But Natasha B. helps women feel better about themselves."

Again everyone shifted in their chairs, gazing up at the ceiling or floor. Dr. Ashworth's smile weakened.

"I'm not saying women *need* to feel better or anything," she continued, her voice speeding up with every word. "I mean, I know we're powerful. It's just that I feel better with . . . shiny lips." Melissa sighed down at the floor. That sounded lame even to her.

"Thank you, Melissa," Dr. Ashworth cut in, obviously afraid that Melissa might continue talking. Melissa wanted to tell her she didn't have to worry, but she couldn't utter another word. She didn't even want to meet the professor's eyes. "So, who's next?" Dr. Ashworth asked, leaning forward to look past Melissa.

Melissa made a motion as if to sit back down, then stopped. She reached down and grabbed her purse. "Excuse me," she muttered, and raced up the main aisle toward the exit.

"See ya, *girls,*" she said over her shoulder as she trotted out the door and across the dark parking lot. She climbed into her car and slammed the door without looking back. Settling against the vinyl seat, she shut her eyes and inhaled the dense air of the car's interior. Was that what she had to look forward to at Smith? Getting mocked by a bunch of know-it-all bookworm types? Guess it didn't matter how many turtlenecks she bought. Obviously she would never fit in there.

She sighed loudly and slumped over onto the steering wheel. So then if she didn't belong at Smith, where exactly did she belong?

"You know, I think you kind of look like her," Trent said, gesturing to the TV screen, where Jennifer Lopez was flashing a worried expression at the camera.

Tia rolled her eyes. "Yeah, right."

"Only you're much better looking."

She picked up a throw pillow and socked him on the chest. "Shut up."

"I mean it, baby." Trent wrapped his arm around her and slowly stroked her arm with his forefinger. "You look more beautiful every day."

"Come on. Stop," Tia said, shrugging his arm off her shoulders. She reached forward, grabbed the remote control, and pressed the volume button. Why did they even bother renting a video if they weren't going to watch it?

She could feel Trent's big brown eyes on her, but she didn't meet his gaze. She knew from experience that he'd be wearing his best hurt-puppy expression, and it wasn't going to work. Not this time.

For some reason, he was really annoying this evening. At the video store he'd snatched up a tape and walked halfway to the front counter before even asking if she wanted to see it. She did, but he could have asked, right? And if he chewed Chee-tos with his mouth open one more time, she was likely to break his jaw.

"Hey. What's with you tonight?" he asked.

Tia finally turned and looked at him. Sure enough, his eyes were all droopy. And there was a spot of cheese powder at the corner of his mouth. "You know, you are so predictable," she said. "Every week we plan a date, and we always end up sitting in your den, watching a video and eating junk food. And halfway into the movie you go all Mr. Smooth on me and compare me to some celebrity as a signal that you want to make out. Tonight it's J. Lo. Last week you said I reminded you of Katie Holmes. The week before it was Jessica Alba. . . ."

"All right, all right." Trent held up a hand. "What's your point exactly?"

She shrugged. "I don't know. Just that . . . it's always the same. You know, some boyfriends and girlfriends do all sorts of cool, different stuff together."

Trent gently grabbed the remote out of her hands and hit the pause button. "Hey," he said, turning back toward her and placing his hands on hers. "I like just hanging with you and getting all cozy like this. I don't need to do lots of cool stuff—I just want to be with you." He reached up and stroked a lock of her long brown hair out of her face. "But if you felt this way, why didn't you just tell me before?"

A jagged lump formed in Tia's throat. As she looked at Trent, she realized she wasn't angry with him. It was as if the irritation she felt was only a thin top layer used to disguise something else. Now it was melting away, revealing all sorts of other bad feelings.

"Because," she replied, her voice cracking. "Because I'm selfish! I'm just an awful, selfish person!" She scowled down at her lap, where her hands were taking turns wringing each other.

"What?" Trent leaned forward, trying to peer

around her curtain of hair. "What are you talking about? You aren't selfish."

Tia let out a snort. "You obviously haven't heard the talk around my school lately."

"About what? Who's talking?"

"Elizabeth and Jade. And probably the rest of my friends too," Tia said, falling back against the sofa cushions. "They're all just mad at me because of this Berkeley thing. They think I should give up my spot so that Evan has a better chance of getting in."

Trent pursed his lips. "But you don't want to, right?"

"I don't know!" Tia threw her hands over her face. "That's just it! I'm so sick of all this college stuff, I don't even know *what* I want!" She let her hands fall back into her lap and slowly leaned sideways, resting her head on Trent's shoulder. "Am I being totally unfair here?" she asked quietly. "Should I just withdraw my name from Berkeley and get this over with?"

"If that's what you want," he murmured. "But I think it has to be your decision. Forget about those other guys. *You* need to decide what's best for *you*— not for anyone else."

"But I don't know if Berkeley is right for me or not," she said. She winced inwardly. When did she become so whiny? It was amazing Trent wasn't totally annoyed with her.

Trent cupped her head in his hands and twisted

around to face her. "Um, Tia? Shouldn't you be finding out if it's right for you? I mean, it is a major decision."

She flashed him a helpless look and then cuddled back up against his chest, letting herself be comforted by his embrace. Trent was right. She wasn't really doing anything to solve this problem. By avoiding making any sort of decision, she was only making things worse.

"You know," she mumbled, "I was supposed to go to this big Berkeley symposium tonight at the civic center. But I blew it off to be with you."

He chuckled. "I'm flattered. But I really think you should go. Besides, we can do this anytime."

Tia sat up and raised an eyebrow at him. "We do it *all* the time," she said, smiling wryly. "Thank you," she murmured, then leaned in for a kiss.

After a long, sweet good-bye Tia grabbed her purse and headed for the door. "You sure it's okay if I leave you like this?" she called over her shoulder.

"Don't worry," he replied, stretching out on the couch and raising the remote. "J. Lo and I will be fine without you."

"Man, oh, man," Evan mumbled as he glanced around the auditorium. He felt simultaneously exhilarated and overwhelmed—the way he used to feel as a small kid when his parents took him to Disneyland (before he became anticorporate).

All around him were tables and makeshift stalls representing some aspect of Berkeley life—from campus organizations to academic departments to student housing. He'd only been at the symposium for half an hour, barely enough time to visit a few booths, but already the university seemed more incredible than he'd ever dreamed. The Amnesty International table had had tons of cool new material. A guy at the Athletics Department booth told him all about a recreational swim team he could go out for. And a social-studies rep gave him all sorts of information on some amazing student exchange programs. Evan felt totally . . . at home.

As he slouched in a corner, trying to decide which booth he should visit next, he caught sight of a poster someone had taped on the wall beside him. Berkeley's Distinguished Lecturer Series, it read. Underneath in red block letters was a short list of some of the speakers they had booked for the upcoming school year. Evan gasped as he read the names.

"Ian Samuels? No way!" he exclaimed.

"You know who that is?"

Evan glanced up and saw a girl sitting on a bench a couple of feet away. She had loads of thick, curly red hair and bright green eyes. She sat cross-legged on the bench with her long cotton skirt draped over her knees.

"Know him? I've only read every single one of his books. He's the only guy who knows what he's talking about when it comes to corporate propaganda."

The girl nodded in amazement. "Did you see who else is speaking this fall? Jim White River."

"Chief White River?" Evan's eyes widened. "He's coming? Oh my God. I love him."

The girl threw back her head and laughed. "You remind me of my twelve-year-old sister when she heard 'N Sync was playing in the next town."

"Yeah, I guess I'm sort of losing it," he said, laughing. "I just can't believe how cool this university is. I can't find anything I don't like."

"I know what you mean," the girl replied with a grin. "I guess it's a good thing we're coming here, then. Looks like all those all-nighters we spent studying are finally paying off." A young guy with a ponytail and scraggly goatee waved at her from the Sierra Club table. She waved back. "Well, I have to go. It was nice talking to you. I'll see you around campus this fall!"

"Uh . . . yeah," he replied as she walked away. "See ya."

Suddenly all of his enthusiasm drained out of him, replaced by heavy dread. What all-nighters? The only time he'd stayed up all night was when he camped out at the Peace Rally last year. He never did it for schoolwork. But he had a feeling Tia probably did.

141

He sighed and slumped back against the wall. Maybe he'd been so busy working for good causes, he'd forgotten to work toward a better future for himself. Maybe Tia did deserve the spot more than he did.

What am I doing? he thought, shaking his head. *Why am I putting myself through this?* He'd been so blown away by the whole "Berkeley experience" that he'd forgotten he hadn't been accepted yet—and maybe never would be. He blew out his breath and ran a hand through his hair. Then he gazed out at the rows and rows of tables and the clusters of excited students milling around them.

Those people were all part of something great, something he wanted to be a part of more than anything. If only he knew how.

Tia sank down onto a wooden bench along the wall of the auditorium. Her feet hurt. Her eyes hurt. And her head was going into information overload.

An hour into her fact-finding mission and she had so far discovered that Berkeley was . . . okay. The Department of Social Work sounded fantastic—even if the rep did use the phrase "social justice" in every other sentence. But most of the popular clubs and groups seemed so political. Several of the people she talked to were really fired up about their causes. It reminded her of the way she got when she cheered for a game, only she got the sense they were intense like that all the time. Compared to them, she felt ignorant and lazy.

I just haven't talked to the right people yet, she told herself as she stretched her legs out in front of her. *After all, I'm not going to college to join clubs—I'm going to study.*

A red banner with the words *Liberal Arts* written on it suddenly caught her eye. It was strung up over two tables on the right-hand side of the auditorium and was surrounded by several lively-looking students.

"Aha," she exclaimed, her smile returning. "There you guys are."

She'd heard so many great things about Berkeley's liberal-arts honors program, which was the main reason she'd applied to the school in the first place. All she had to do was talk to one of their representatives about their degree requirements. That ought to help her decide once and for all.

Tia stood and headed in the direction of the banner. Judging by all the happy, excited-looking people swarming the booth, it seemed like liberal arts was *the* department to be in. She quickened her step. Maybe that's where she belonged too. Maybe this was the grand plan all along—that she was destined to discover her future tonight as a Berkeley liberal-arts major.

Once she arrived at the table, she had to wait a few

minutes for a rep to become available. Eventually a cute, twenty-something guy wearing jeans and a Berkeley sweatshirt turned toward her and smiled. "Hi. I'm John," he said, pointing to the stick-on name tag just under his left shoulder.

"I'm Tia," she said, shaking his hand. "Do you have any information on your honors program?"

"Ah," he said, raising his eyebrows. "You want the hard stuff, huh?" He handed her a thick, parchment-colored brochure. "It's the best program of its kind in this part of the country—if not the whole country."

"Really?" Tia smiled down at the booklet in her hand. A fluttery feeling began in her stomach. So far, she liked the sound of this. "So what are the requirements?"

John reached over and flipped a few pages in her brochure. "Right here," he said, pointing.

Tia glanced down at the list and gasped. The honors program had twice as many course requirements as the other plans she'd looked at.

"What's wrong?" John asked.

"Uh, nothing. Just . . . is this a four-year degree plan? Or six year?"

John laughed. "No, it's a four-year plan, I promise. Pretty impressive, huh?"

"But don't they let you take other stuff too?" she asked. "You know, like non-liberal-arts courses?"

"Sure." John shrugged. "I mean, you don't get to take as many electives as the other degree plans allow, but you get some."

Tia sighed. She'd been hoping she could explore a bit and take a few different types of electives to help her decide what to do with her life—as well as just some fun stuff. But it hardly seemed possible under this plan. Maybe the people who signed up for the honors degree had no interest in pursuing anything else.

She squinted at the list again. "What do these *W's* mean next to the classes?"

"It stands for 'writing intensive,'" John explained. "Those are classes that require either a semester-long term paper or a major essay every couple of weeks or so."

Tia's jaw dropped open. "Every couple of weeks?" she repeated. "Are honors majors not allowed to go on dates or sleep more than four hours a night?"

John chuckled only slightly. Tia could tell he wasn't all that amused. "It's an excellent program, and it teaches you a lot. But it isn't the easiest plan on campus."

"Okay," she said, nodding. "Thanks a lot for your help." She turned and shuffled away. The exhilaration she'd felt earlier had completely disappeared. Now she just felt tired. And disappointed. And lost.

Obviously the liberal-arts honors program wasn't for her after all. Did that mean Berkeley wasn't either?

Evan Plummer

I'm used to fighting the powers that be. I'm not afraid. I've staged protests on every topic you can imagine. I've marched, chanted, picketed, circulated petitions, sang songs, boycotted "tainted" products, and been in my share of riots. I've even been teargassed. I think if something is important enough, you should be willing to do anything you can for it.

Only . . . I can't do any of those things for me right now. I can't raise my fist at Berkeley or collect signatures or urge people not to go there. None of my tactics will help me get into the school, and that makes things even worse. Because beyond all the anger and frustration at not being admitted to Berkeley, I feel totally helpless.

I'd rather face tear gas any day.

CHAPTER

Passport to a New Life

9

"How was the seminar, sweetie?" Melissa's mother asked her the second she walked into the house. Her mom had been practically dancing around the house since Melissa told her she was going to Smith. Now she wished she hadn't said anything.

"Oh, fine," Melissa replied with effort. She was in no mood to tell the real truth. Her parents would find out soon enough that she wouldn't be going there after all. But for now, she'd rather not relive that nightmare.

"What's wrong?" Her mother peered closely at her. "You look tired."

"I am," she replied. At least that wasn't a lie. She really did feel worn out—as if she'd finally come back down to earth after a week of jetting around the stratosphere. She slipped off her jacket and kept moving. "It was lots and lots of talking and stuff, and I'm completely exhausted. So I'll probably just turn in now. Good night."

"Good night," she heard her mother call after her as she sped up the stairs to her room.

Once inside the safety of her bedroom, she closed the door and leaned back against it, sinking to the floor and shutting her eyes. A shaky feeling spread through her whole body, and her fingers and toes tingled. She recognized the sensations—the signals her body sent when she was on the verge of losing her grip. If she wasn't careful, pretty soon she'd have no control over what happened next.

How did things go so wrong so fast? She hadn't realized how crucial her plan of going to Smith had become. Now that it had fizzled, she had nothing. Nothing for her now, and nothing to look forward to.

Stop thinking like that, she told herself as she hugged her knees to her chest. *You've got a future. You'll still go to college somewhere.*

Only that didn't help her now. Right now she had no friends, no power, no plan—nothing to focus on. She'd never felt this abandoned and vulnerable. Not even the last time when the dark thoughts had taken control, when she'd been afraid that she'd lost Will forever.

Will. A sudden image of his face flashed in her mind. Will had called. He had been worried about her. Maybe he was even trying to get back together, in his own way. But she hadn't been able to hear him because she was still so angry.

Melissa's breathing gradually slowed. Will had been her lifeline for so long. With him around, she always felt she could handle anything. They hadn't always been good to each other, but they'd always instinctively met each other's unspoken needs—like some sort of protective coating that found the cracks and filled them in, strengthening and completing the other person.

She loved Will. She *needed* him. Maybe it wasn't too late to get him back. After all, it sounded like he missed her. And he'd actually left a basketball game to check up on her. That had to mean something. There might still be a way to make things up to him.

Melissa stood up straight and pulled her car keys from her purse. At least she knew where she belonged now—with Will.

"Forget it," Tia mumbled as she stood back against the wall away from the boisterous symposium crowd. "This party is officially over."

She'd given Berkeley a real chance. She'd talked to all sorts of people and read up on all the clubs and programs, but she just couldn't picture herself there. None of the organizations interested her. The degree programs didn't fit her needs either. She'd even read a poster bragging about all the distinguished people giving speeches at the university this fall—and she didn't recognize a single name. The clincher, though, was when she'd asked someone behind the Health and Physical Education table about getting on the cheerleading squad and the woman had actually given her a "look."

In a way, she was really glad she'd come. It helped her discover beyond a doubt that Berkeley wasn't her thing. Now all she wanted to do was race back to Trent and see if there were any Chee-tos left.

Tia looked around for the nearest exit sign. Suddenly she caught sight of a familiar figure. Evan.

He was leaning with his hands on the Green Party table, nodding along as he listened to the student rep. It was amazing how comfortable he seemed. Almost as if he'd been a part of this scene his whole life—as if he belonged.

A smile slowly made its way across her face. Berkeley might not be the right place for her, but it was *definitely* the right place for Evan. He deserved to go here, and she was going to do whatever she could to help out.

Tia walked over and tapped him on the shoulder. "Hi," she said.

Evan whirled around. "Um . . . hi," he said, his features immediately creasing with worry.

"Can we talk for a sec?" Tia asked, motioning toward a quiet spot by a window.

"Sure," he replied. "Hey, I'll catch you later," he said to the Green Party guy as he followed Tia. As soon as they reached the semiseclusion of the small window, he shoved his hands into the pockets of his parka and hunched his shoulders. "Listen, um, I really wasn't trying to cheat you out of your spot or anything. I get that you worked hard for it, and you deserve a shot to go for it if it's what you want." He paused, avoiding her gaze. "I just came to check the place out. You know, just in case."

"I know," Tia said, nodding.

Evan raised his eyes to meet hers. "So what do you say? Truce?" He held his right hand out toward her.

"Sure, truce," Tia said, grasping his palm and shaking it. "But I've been doing some thinking too. People kept saying stuff to me, acting like *I* stole the spot from *you*. After all, you are so the Berkeley type. And I am so not."

"Sure you are," he said. "You'll see. You're going to love it there. You'll find your thing and—"

"No, Evan. I won't," she interrupted. "Because I'm not going to Berkeley."

Evan's eyes widened. "What?"

"I realized that tonight. Berkeley isn't right for me." She gazed out at the collection of people and booths. "But it *is* for you. So first thing tomorrow morning I'm telling Mr. Nelson I'm withdrawing my name. And hopefully that will help bump you off the waiting list."

"You . . . ? You're not . . . ?" Evan's face drained of color. He stood there gaping at her for several seconds.

"Hey, are you all right?" she asked, laughing.

"Oh, man. I don't believe this," he said finally, shaking his head. He broke into a huge grin, his brown eyes gleaming. "Thank you." He reached over, snatched her up in a hug, and spun her around a couple of times before setting her back down again. "Thank you!" he said again.

"You're welcome," Tia said, still laughing. She pushed her hair back out of her eyes and enjoyed taking in the pure happiness radiating from Evan's face.

She definitely felt better. Of course, she still had no idea what she would do after high school, but it felt good to help Evan get where he belonged. Plus she was glad she hadn't lost a friend.

Will frowned as he walked through the foyer to his front door, wondering who would be showing up at their house at this hour on a Wednesday night. He gave the peephole a quick check before opening the door and felt a jumble of mixed emotions rush through him.

Melissa.

He took a deep breath, then opened the door. Melissa stood on his front porch, a cool smile on her face. "Hi, Will," she said, looking unbelievably calm.

"What do you want?" he asked, fighting to keep his voice neutral.

Melissa slipped her hand out from behind her back and held it out to him. Two long, gold-colored tickets stuck out of her grasp. "They're for the Lakers game tomorrow night," she said with a sly grin.

Will blinked, studying the tickets. Sure enough, they were for tomorrow night's Lakers game against the Portland Blazers. He'd been really excited to see that matchup. Melissa would know that. She knew practically everything about him. Of course, she knew how to take advantage of that knowledge too.

"What's this for?" he asked flatly, restraining himself from plucking the tickets from her fist.

She shrugged. "I just wanted to apologize. It was nice of you to call last night. I'm sorry I reamed you out. I was just—" She paused and shrugged again, watching him closely with her pale blue eyes. "I was just stressed out about schoolwork."

I'll bet, he thought. Still, it made a small difference to hear her admit she was wrong. Maybe she'd finally realized how out of line her stupid plan with Aaron had been. He leaned up against the door frame and waited for her to finish. "And?" he prompted when she didn't go on.

Her smug smile disappeared. "And what?"

153

Will frowned. "Aren't you going to say you're sorry for messing around with Aaron?"

Melissa's features hardened. "Why don't we just consider ourselves even," she muttered.

"Even?" Will repeated, straightening up and glaring at her. "What are you talking about?"

"Hey, you fooled around with Erika Brooks, didn't you?" she replied calmly. "I only did the Aaron thing to get back at you for that."

Will shook his head. "You can't even compare them. What happened with me was totally different. I didn't mean for it to happen. You *planned* to cheat on me—with *Aaron*. You're so low, you'd even use our friends to get revenge."

"What's the matter, Will? Feel like you can't trust me? Feel like I've ripped your heart out? Well, guess what?" She tilted her head and fixed him with a cold, hard stare. "That's exactly how I felt when I saw you with Erika. Seems no different to me."

Will's eyes narrowed and his jaw clenched so tightly, he could almost feel his teeth crack. There she went again, acting like she was the victim. How many times had he fallen for this? He didn't even want to try and count the instances when she'd twisted things around and acted all hurt and bitter until *he* ended up apologizing for *her* mistakes.

And he was letting her get to him again. As soon

as he'd seen her on his porch, he should have told her to get lost. Obviously she thought she could bring him gifts and pretend to be all wounded so he'd come crawling back to her. Well, she could forget it. He wasn't falling for her tricks anymore.

"You know what? You can keep your lousy Lakers tickets," he hissed. "You can quit cheerleading, you can throw yourself at guys—you can drop out of high school for all I care. From now on I just want you to *leave me alone!*" With that, he stepped back inside the house and slammed the door as hard as he could.

There! he thought, stalking down the hall to his room. Maybe now he could finally put Melissa behind him. He did feel different somehow. Ready for his future at NYU.

All he needed to do was mail that acceptance letter. Then there would be no turning back. He'd be committed to a life without Melissa.

Will stomped over to his desk and rummaged through the top drawer. Nothing. He searched the rest of the drawers. Nothing. "What the . . . ?" he muttered. Will looked all over his room—the shelves, the floor, inside books, under the bed, even in his closet. But the NYU letter was nowhere.

Great, he thought as he sank down on the edge of his bed. Here he was finally ready to start over, and his passport to a new life ended up missing.

To: Parent Guest List *(blind cc)*
From: stevewake@cal.rr.com
Re: Surprise bash

Hello, all! Please excuse the mass electronic mail out, but we wanted to reach as many people as we could as quickly as possible. As you may know, my parents will be celebrating their 25th wedding anniversary tomorrow and, thanks to my kid sister, a surprise dinner has been arranged at Le Chateau at 7 P.M. We hope all of you can attend. If you have any questions, please call Elizabeth on her private line: 555-6742.

                              Sincerely yours,
                              Steven

Little Miss Perfect

Will trudged into the kitchen Thursday afternoon, his whole body exhausted. Today had been one of those days when all he wanted was to hear the final bell, and it seemed like every class lasted forever.

"Will?"

Will glanced over and saw his father sitting at the kitchen table. Mr. Simmons's hands were clasped in front of him, and deep lines stood out on his forehead and around his eyes.

Uh-oh, Will thought, surveying the scene. His stomach tightened into a million knots. He hadn't seen his father look this worried —other than when Will was in the hospital himself—since Melissa had tried to commit suicide in the fall.

"What is it?" Will asked, his throat getting dry. "What happened?"

"Sit down." His father motioned to the chair opposite him.

Will swallowed hard. He barely felt himself sink

157

down into the seat. "What's wrong, Dad?" he asked, bracing himself. Maybe Melissa had tried something again. It was all his fault. He had been really harsh with her yesterday. And he'd sensed that she was in a bad place, underneath the act. He should have been more careful.

His father sighed, took off his glasses, and rubbed his eyes. "I know it's been hard for you lately," he began as he readjusted his glasses. "I know it's been tough to think of yourself as 'Joe College' this fall instead of 'College Football Star.' And I wonder if you're ready to face that future."

Will frowned, feeling both relieved and confused. Obviously this wasn't about Melissa. But what *was* his dad trying to tell him? "Dad, I already have my future locked," he said. "You know I'm going to NYU. All I have to do is mail off the acceptance letter."

"Then what's stopping you?" his dad asked, looking him right in the eye.

For a moment Will just sat there, speechless. Then he gave a small shrug and stared down at the tabletop. "I, um . . . I can't find it," he confessed meekly.

Will waited for the torrent of shouts his father was sure to hurl at him. He didn't care. He deserved it. It was pretty lame of him to lose something that important. He only hoped they could call up NYU and ask them to send another.

But his father didn't scream. Instead he pushed himself back from the table, stood, and motioned with his hand for Will to follow. Will got up and walked over to the refrigerator with him. With a quick glance at Will, Mr. Simmons opened the freezer door, reached in, and pulled out Will's acceptance letter—frozen stiff.

Oh. So *that's* where he'd put it. He flashed his father a helpless look. "I must have accidentally left it there when I was getting some ice cream," he explained. "I guess I've been a little out of it lately."

"A little?" his father repeated. "Son, are you sure NYU is really where you want to go? For years you'd planned on a college-sports career, and that's only recently been taken away from you. Maybe you aren't ready to admit that yet."

"No," Will said firmly. "I am ready. Look." He snatched the letter from his father's grasp and pointed to it. "It's all filled out and everything. All it needs is a stamp. Remember when I asked you for one?"

His father whipped his wallet out of his back pocket and pulled out a book of stamps. "Here you go," he said, handing it to Will. "Now there's nothing to stop you. You could walk down the street and mail that now." He folded his arms across his chest and leaned back against the counter, watching Will intently.

Will felt like he was being dared. "Maybe I should," he replied, lifting his chin defiantly.

"Well?" Mr. Simmons gestured toward the back door. "What are you waiting for?"

"Nothing. I just—" Will paused. What *was* he waiting for? He had everything he needed. He should just march down and throw the letter in the mailbox. That would show his dad. "Nothing," he repeated. "I'm going."

Will peeled off a stamp and stuck it on the top-right-hand corner of the envelope. Then he grabbed his jacket and headed out the door.

The sun was starting to dip behind the trees, making everything cool and shadowy. Will headed down the sidewalk in the direction of the mailbox.

His dad was so off base. Just because Will had held off mailing the NYU letter didn't mean he was afraid to go. He'd just been busy dealing with stuff, that was all. Of course he wanted to go to NYU. So what if he wouldn't be a big sports star? He didn't care. So what if he didn't know anyone there? He'd meet people. So what if it was completely opposite what he and Melissa had planned for so long? If she could blow him off to go to Massachusetts, he could definitely go off to New York without her . . . right?

Will's gait gradually dwindled into small, dragging baby steps. The melting letter was making his hands wet and clammy. Looming in front of him, just across the street, he could see the large, rounded mailbox. He stopped walking and stared at it. The slot for the letters resembled a fixed, grim mouth. *It doesn't want the letter,* he thought. *It doesn't want me to mail this.*

He stared down at the envelope. *New York City,* the address read. *New York.* It just seemed so far away. He tried to picture himself walking the busy sidewalks, sitting inside a deli, or heading up and down the steps to the subway—but he couldn't. A few nights before he had taken out a map of the United States and measured the distance between Manhattan and Northampton, Massachusetts, where Smith College was. It was two inches away on the map—162 miles in real life. *Exactly 162 miles,* he thought, shaking his head. Close enough for occasional visits, but too far for a relationship.

Relationship? What was he doing considering a long-distance relationship with Melissa? What was wrong with him?

But he already knew the answer: "I need her," he mumbled aloud.

That was why he hadn't mailed the letter yet. His dad had been right about one thing. He *was* avoiding going to NYU, but not because of some ruined athletic career. He just didn't want to be so far from Liss.

Sure, they had their problems. Big ones. But he'd

always known she was the only one he could really be with. He needed her. He loved her.

Instead of crossing the street to the mailbox, Will veered right, his pace fast and determined again. He'd run out of excuses. It would take a while to reach Melissa's house on foot, but he couldn't go home and face his dad without mailing the letter. Besides, if he didn't see her soon, he might end up "accidentally" setting the stupid thing on fire.

Jessica took a bite of her chicken cordon bleu and settled back against the plush velvet-backed dining chair, savoring the taste. The food was absolutely perfect. In fact, everything was.

She glanced down the long, rectangular table at the rest of the assembled guests. On her left, her parents sat sipping wine and gazing into each other's eyes like blissed-out newlyweds. On the other side of them sat Steven, who kept tugging on his tie every few seconds but otherwise seemed to be having a great time. To Jessica's right, Elizabeth sat twiddling her fork in her steamed vegetables. Her eyes had that far-off, wistful look, and Jessica could tell she was thinking about Jeff. He'd had to work tonight and couldn't be with her, but at least Elizabeth had managed to be pleasant and excited around her parents and the guests.

"What a beautiful dinner!" Mrs. Applegate sat across the table, talking with her husband. "Don't you think so, Hal? Isn't this all just so beautiful?"

Jessica beamed. She dabbed the sides of her mouth with her cloth napkin and gazed around Le Chateau's private dining room. It really was nice. She had to congratulate herself on a job well done. Gerard, the maître d', had seen to the entire list of details she'd left him—the menu, the table arrangement, the dim lighting and soft jazz music. He'd even remembered her saying that gladioli were her mother's favorite flower and placed several tall, slender vases full of deep purple blooms along the table. Gerard certainly deserved a huge thank-you. In fact, she did too. It felt good to know that because of her quick thinking, her parents were having the coolest, most romantic anniversary they could have asked for.

"That Steven is such a wonderful boy," Mrs. Applegate went on. "I don't know how he pulled this off, considering how busy he must be with college."

Steven? Jessica scowled. Steven hardly did a thing. She considered clarifying everything for Mrs. Applegate but decided not to. Mrs. Applegate was a little kooky. Everyone else probably knew the real story.

"Oh, I know," Mrs. Barber chimed in from Mrs. Applegate's left. "Steven has always been so considerate.

I'm sure Ned and Alice are so proud of him."

Jessica could feel her cheeks burning. She glanced over at Elizabeth to see if she'd overheard, but as usual her twin was off in la-la land, tracing hearts into the sauce on her plate.

"Steven thought of everything too." Mrs. Covington, who was sitting on the other side of Mrs. Barber, had joined their conversation. The three ladies sat huddled together in their own private semicircle. "I noticed he had cordon bleu served, which is Ned's favorite, and he even remembered to have gladioli for Alice."

"Isn't he a sweetheart?"

"What a thoughtful boy!"

Jessica wanted to retch. She briefly entertained the idea of tossing her plate of cordon bleu, Frisbee-like, into the ladies' laps. But she quickly pushed the thought from her mind. It wasn't those biddies' fault they were so mixed up about who planned the whole evening. They probably just assumed it had been Steven since he was the one who contacted them all.

Still, it *would* be nice to get some recognition. Maybe she could find a reason to give Steven a pop quiz over his parents' favorite foods and flowers. She smiled at the image of her brother stuttering and sweating in front of everyone.

"Excuse me? Everyone, would you excuse me for a moment?"

Jessica glanced up to see her father rise from his seat, tapping his spoon against the side of his wineglass.

"I just wanted to say a few words of thanks."

Jessica sat up straight. *Yes!* she cheered silently. Now she would *finally* get some recognition.

The guests gradually grew silent and smiled at him expectantly. Mr. Wakefield cleared his throat. "I think a lot of you knew me twenty-five years ago," he said, looking off into the distance as if gazing back in time. "I had a lot more hair then."

The guests chuckled appreciatively.

"And energy."

More chuckles.

"And a little less of other things." He patted his stomach lightly.

Everyone laughed, including Jessica.

"But I wasn't what you would call . . . fulfilled," he went on. "Then I met Alice." He looked over at Mrs. Wakefield, and his smile turned brighter, yet more private. "She changed all that. Once I met her, I had everything. She's taught me so much about love and family and even myself. For that I'm grateful. And she's given me three wonderful children." His arm swept around toward Jessica, Elizabeth, and Steven. "For that, I'm exhausted."

The crowd laughed. Steven shouted, "Hey!"

"*And* grateful," Mr. Wakefield added, grinning slyly. "So here's to my beautiful, special wife." He turned toward Mrs. Wakefield and raised his glass. "Honey, thank you for putting up with me for all these years. You have made me the luckiest man in the world. I love you."

"Awww," the guests cooed collectively. Tears sprang into the corners of Jessica's eyes, and she had to blink rapidly to prevent her makeup from smearing. She glanced over at her mother and grinned. Mrs. Wakefield was staring affectionately at her husband. Her mouth was curled in a soft smile, and her eyes were wide and watery.

Everyone clapped as Mr. Wakefield drained his glass and sat back down. Jessica couldn't be too upset he hadn't thanked her for planning the dinner. After all, he'd made Mom so happy with his sweet speech.

"My turn," Mrs. Wakefield called out as she stood.

Jessica clapped along with everyone else. Now she was sure to be acknowledged. Her dad could be a little clueless at times, but her mother always remembered important gestures like that.

"First I have to say how much I am enjoying this special evening," she said. The others clapped and shouted their consent.

Here it comes, Jessica thought. Now all their

friends would know what a thoughtful daughter she was. And responsible too. Maybe Steven would even stop calling her Airhead.

"I am very grateful to my in-laws, who I understand are graciously footing the bill, even though they couldn't join us this evening," Mrs. Wakefield continued. She turned toward Mr. Wakefield and raised her glass. "To you, sweetheart, for making each day warm, meaningful, and never ever dull. I love you, honey." The crowd murmured "oohs" of approval. "And . . ." She turned completely around and raised her glass in Jessica's direction. Jessica held her breath. The butterflies in her stomach seemed to be turning somersaults. "To my wonderful kids, whom I love dearly, for planning this beautiful evening. What a feat! I'm sure Elizabeth probably went through twenty different to-do lists."

The guests chuckled. "Hear, hear," they shouted with raised glasses, most of them directed toward Elizabeth.

Jessica sat frozen in place, her eyes wide with horror. Did she hear right? Did her mother just credit *Elizabeth* for doing most of the work? If anyone should have been singled out, it was her!

She glanced back up at her mother, waiting for her to continue, but Mrs. Wakefield simply sat back down and began chatting with a couple of guests across the table. Jessica's heart sank. Just because Elizabeth had the task—her *only* task, and an easy one at that—of getting her parents to the restaurant that night, they probably automatically assumed she planned everything. And the guests had been giving Steven all the credit. That meant everyone here probably figured Space Case Jessica never lifted a finger—that she just came along for the ride.

But of course they'd believe that. Elizabeth had always been the "responsible" twin. Jessica was the loser. She was the selfish one, the boy-crazy one, the one you couldn't count on.

A lump rose up inside her throat, and she could tell the tears would be there any second. "Excuse me," she whispered to no one in particular as she pushed back her chair and ran out of the room.

"Jessica?" Elizabeth watched her twin disappear from the dining room as fast as she could manage in her black three-inch heels.

Uh-oh. If she were Jessica, she'd be upset too. It really wasn't fair for Mom and Dad to overlook her like that. Of course, they had no idea Jessica had practically planned the whole party. No one had really told them—not yet. She had planned to brag on Jessica during dinner, but after the big initial "surprise," she'd sort of forgotten. All the talk about romance and

168

relationships kept reminding her of Jeff.

Maybe she should go after Jessica and talk to her.

Elizabeth quietly rose from her seat and walked out of the room. She pushed open the coral-colored door to the ladies' room. There, sitting against the back wall, was Jessica. Her knees were pulled up to her chest and her head was down, but she was obviously crying.

"Jess?" Elizabeth said softly as she crept closer.

Jessica didn't respond. Her back heaved up and down with each shuddery sob.

"Jess, I'm sorry about what Mom said," Elizabeth tried. "I mean . . . about what she didn't say." She knelt down next to Jessica and placed a hand on her arm. "I promise I'll set them straight. I'll tell them about all the stuff you did."

Jessica glanced up. "It . . . doesn't . . . matter . . . now," she choked out. "It's . . . too . . . late!" The last word was stretched out into a long wail, and Jessica slumped back over, weeping.

Elizabeth winced at the sound of her sobs. She couldn't remember seeing her sister this upset in a long time. Was this really about the dinner? Or was something else wrong?

She tried to think of something that might calm her down. "It's going to be all right," she said lamely, patting Jessica's arm. "Do you want me to go get Mom?"

"No," came Jessica's muffled reply.

"You know, I think Steven's getting kind of bored," she said with a feeble chuckle. "You want me to get him to drive you home?"

"No!"

Elizabeth blew out her breath and sat down on the cold tile floor next to Jessica. "I don't understand," she said, pulling her skirt down over her legs. "What's really upsetting you?"

Jessica didn't respond. Elizabeth sat listening to her sister's crying as patiently as she could. As bad as she felt for her sister, she was also starting to get a little annoyed. It was just like Jessica to go all dramatic during their parents' big bash. Was everything always about her?

"Excuse me? Is there an Elizabeth Wakefield in here?"

Elizabeth looked up to see one of the hostesses poking her head inside the ladies' room. The woman glanced around the room until she spotted Elizabeth and Jessica sitting against the back wall. Her eyebrows flew up in a disapproving stare.

"That's me," Elizabeth said, raising her hand like a third grader during roll call. "I mean, I'm Elizabeth."

The hostess pointed over her shoulder. "There's a call on hold for you," she said, a tinge of irritation in her voice. "Some man named Jeff?"

170

Elizabeth automatically leaped to her feet, a smile popping onto her face. "Okay. Thanks. I'll be right there." The hostess backed out of the doorway and disappeared. Elizabeth took a couple of steps toward the exit. "I'll be back in a minute. Will you be okay, Je—?" She spun around to look at Jessica and stopped in midsentence.

Jessica's head was raised, revealing her red, blotchy face as she stared angrily at Elizabeth. "*This* is what's upsetting me," she said hoarsely with a gesture toward the door. "This is exactly the problem."

Elizabeth frowned. "What are you talking about? What's the problem?"

"You!" came Jessica's shrill reply. "Whenever anyone else needs you—Jeff, the *Scope,* even Evan Plummer—you drop everything to help them. You're right there for everyone *except me!*" Her voice choked into a sob, and tears streamed down her face again.

"*What?*" Elizabeth replied, totally shocked by her sister's accusation. Why was she suddenly the bad guy? Just because she had a boyfriend who liked to check up on her? She'd tried to be here for Jessica, but the girl obviously didn't want to be helped. Now Jessica was turning on her? "Don't get all worked up about this, Jess. This has nothing to do with you."

"It never does!" Jessica shouted, jumping to her

171

feet. "I never matter in the family. All these years I've been the flaky, airheaded twin who no one takes seriously. And you've always been Little Miss Perfect who never does anything wrong. Only guess what. Now you're the flake." She raised her arm and pointed at Elizabeth. "You get to space out about stuff and no one calls you on it. *Me?* I bust my butt trying to organize a party for Mom and Dad and no one—not Mom, not Dad, not Steven, not you—*no one* says thank you!"

Elizabeth felt more than a small twinge of guilt. Jessica was right. She hadn't thanked her—at least, not yet. And she had been brushing her off a lot lately too. It was only because she was so busy with stuff. Important stuff. But then . . . maybe that was Jessica's point. She was important too.

"Hey, Jess," Elizabeth began, her voice low. "I really—"

"Save it!" Jessica snapped, her red, puffy eyes flashing. She stalked past Elizabeth and threw open the rest-room door. "Go talk to your boyfriend!" she yelled before marching back into the restaurant.

Dingdong.

"Mom, get the door!" Melissa shouted from her sprawled position on the sofa.

Her mom didn't answer. Other than the swelling

music from the dippy TV movie Melissa was watching, the house was completely silent.

Great. Her mom was probably in the shower already. And Dad was out of town. That meant she was the only one around to do anything. Of course, she could just ignore whoever it was and they'd eventually go away.

Dingdong.

For some reason, the doorbell sounded louder, more urgent. Melissa groaned and put a throw pillow over her ear. She did not want to interact with the world right now. The world was full of people with real lives, complete with friends and exciting careers and doting significant others. Her life, on the other hand, was basically a dud. It already took an extreme focus on schoolwork, chores, and lame television to avoid drowning in self-pity. One more in-your-face reminder of how bad things were and she was liable to lose it.

Dingdong. Dingdong.

Ugh. Whoever it was obviously wasn't going to give up. They could probably see the lights and hear the TV.

Melissa forced herself to sit up. Then she sighed and stood. It was probably someone collecting money for a charity. Some of those people didn't get the idea unless you slammed the door in their faces.

Actually, that might feel good, she thought as she walked toward the door. After all, why should she give to others when everyone else in the world had already abandoned *her*?

Melissa threw open the door. "Look, whatever it is, we're not interest—" She froze midsentence when she saw who it was.

Will stood on her front stoop, facing her. An awkward half smile cut across his face, and his hands were tugging nervously on the edges of a large envelope. Melissa couldn't help noticing the New York University logo, and her chest grew tight. Had he actually come all the way here just to rub it in her face that he was going to college in New York without her?

"Hey," he said. He shot a quick glance at her face, then his eyes darted back down and he stared at his feet.

"Hey," she said back, crossing her arms over her chest. He didn't seem like he was gloating . . . so why did he bring that NYU envelope here?

"Listen, I'm . . . um . . . I'm sorry about the whole basketball-ticket thing," he mumbled, his eyes jumping from her face to the ground and back to her face. "Everything's been so crazy."

"Yeah," she said. She leaned against the doorway for support.

They were both quiet. Melissa wasn't about to

venture one more word until she knew why he was here. Finally, after a seemingly endless silence, he took a step back and turned as if to go. "Well, I guess I should . . ."

"Wait!" The word was out of Melissa's mouth before she realized it. Taking a deep breath, she tried to force some calm into her voice. "I . . . um . . . I see you've got your NYU letter," she said, pointing lamely at the envelope. "You know, I'm happy for you—that you got accepted. It's a really good school."

Will frowned down at the envelope in his grasp. "Yeah. It's great," he said.

A tiny warm spot of hope flickered inside her. He didn't sound at all excited.

"And you'll do great at Smith too," he added, meeting her gaze.

Melissa stared into his clear blue eyes. That tiny warm spot started to spread, easing every muscle in her body. Muscles that seemed to have been tensed for so long, she couldn't even remember when they *hadn't* been.

That's it, she thought. *No more games.* She was going to try telling the truth for a change. "I'm not going to Smith," she blurted.

Will's eyes widened. "You're not?"

She shook her head. "I just realized it's not right for me."

"Oh," he said, nodding. For the first time he looked right at her without quickly glancing away. "So . . . where will you go?"

Melissa felt an actual smile tug at her lips. This was good. This was very, very good. Maybe now that the silly clumsiness had disappeared, she could take another, bolder risk.

"I don't know," she replied. "Think you could sell me on NYU?"

"Actually," he began, ducking his head sheepishly, "I'm probably not going. I decided I really didn't want to be so far away from . . . stuff."

"Oh," she said, feeling warmer by the second. "So, um . . . do you want to come inside and maybe talk about, you know, college and stuff?" She held her breath as she watched him closely. Time seemed to slow down.

Slowly a smile crept across Will's face. "Sure, I think I—"

Before he'd even finished speaking, Melissa bolted across the porch and threw her arms around him, burying her face in his chest. He reached down and pulled her even closer, holding her tight. For a long time they just stood there, embracing. Melissa closed her eyes and breathed in the familiar scent of his cologne. She could almost feel the rhythm of their heartbeats combining into one strong, steady beat. Eventually she leaned backward and locked her gaze with his.

"I guess we should go in," she said, gesturing toward the door. "We've got a lot of things to figure out."

Will shrugged, still smiling. "Okay. But we don't have to figure everything out just yet," he murmured. "We've got the rest of our lives to do that."

Our lives, Melissa repeated to herself as they stepped into the house arm in arm. She definitely liked the sound of that.

JESSICA WAKEFIELD
8:37 P.M.

It's bad enough when strange salesclerks don't take you seriously and don't want you around. But what about when it's your own family?

ELIZABETH WAKEFIELD
9:22 P.M.

Jessica has totally lost it. She's beyond hysterics. I guess everyone's been a little distracted lately, and she hasn't gotten the attention she craves.

Something tells me we're really in for it now.

WILL SIMMONS
9:34 P.M.

Okay, so I went back to Liss. Does that make me a wuss?

I still don't know where I'm going to school or what I want to do or how I'm even going to face my friends at school. But I did figure something out: <u>I need Melissa.</u> Sometimes I don't want to need her —if that makes sense— but I do. And since that's the only thing perfectly clear to me right now, I'm going for it.

She and I have a lot of stuff to work on, but I'm willing to tough it out. And if you ask me, that's not something a total wuss would do.

JADE WU
9:36 P.M.

Evan just called to say that Tia was withdrawing her name from Berkeley— I'm so psyched for him. I wonder what finally brought that girl to her senses?

I went to Mom's bedroom to use the computer so I could e-mail him a romantic message, but the door was locked. I don't know what's up with her lately—she was there when I got home from school, and she didn't come out for dinner. She just keeps saying she's "working on something." I wish she would tell me what.

Anyway, right now I'm just really happy for Evan. Of course, now I need to figure out where I'm going to go to college. . . .